Heroes and Monsters

Ten Tales in Verse

I0555466

Dharanidhar Sahu

© 2007 by Lin Publications
All rights reserved.

ISBN - 978-0-6151-7589-8

Printed in the United States of America.

*For
the new comers to the
family.*

*Lolo
Sonu &
Lin*

Contents

1   The King and the Cook   6

2   The Cyclopes and Odysseus   24

3   The Sirens and Orpheus   32

4   The Sleepless Dragon and Jason   42

5   The Hydra and Hercules   52

6   The Gorgon Medusa and Perseus   61

7   The Minotaur and Theseus   74

8   The Chimaera and Bellerophon   81

9   The Sphinx and Oedipus   89

10   The Story of the Centaurs   94

About the Book

The monsters are conundrums in God's creation;
Their contrary features defy a clear classification.
To all those monsters, certain things are common:
They have peculiar features that cause confusion;
They possess magical powers, and, what is more,
For each of those monsters there is always a hero
Who would either kill or disable it sooner or later.

Each monster is invariably gifted with a disparate
Physiognomy, an anatomical combo of this or that,
Limbs of multifarious beasts, as if Mother Nature
Who was then in an inchoate state of procreation,
Was tinkering with life-forms, hence did engender
A woman with eagle's wings and the body of a lion;
Women with serpentine bodies; the body of a man
With a bullhead; a race, half equine, half human;
A lion with a goat's head having for its tail a python;
A single eye in the forehead; crazy flowers in tares;
Women born old; hags with live serpents for hairs.

The hero and the monster stand for opposite poles:
The first represents Order, the second, the Chaos.
This book narrates the story of ten noted monsters,
And that of as many heroes equal to their powers.
Each tale pans out the making of one such monster,
Its depredations, ending with its ultimate surrender
To the evolutionary principle embodied in the hero.

In the feudal times, a resourceful cook Naga Singh
Tantalizes a heaven-obsessed and monstrous king;
While seemingly satisfying that king's own desire,
He sends him packing to a paradisiacal hereafter.
Polyphemus, one of the huge, single-eyed Cyclopes,
Is shrewdly disabled by the Homeric hero Odysseus.
Physically comely, but insidious-voiced Siren sisters
Are turned innocuous by the ace musician Orpheus;
The Greek prince Jason acquires the Golden Fleece
By outmaneuvering the Sleepless Dragon of Colchis;

The Chimaera, a composite of goat, python and lion,
Is attacked and killed by Pegasus-riding Bellerophon;
Noble Perseus beheads Medusa, the mortal Gorgon.
The Hydra of Lerna is hacked and burnt by Hercules;
The Sphinx, who held to ransom the state of Thebes,
Is outwitted and consequently destroyed by Oedipus;
Theseus enters the Labyrinth and slays the Minotaur;
Atalanta, Theseus and Hercules kill many a Centaur.

These events, culled from the works of Apollodorus,
Homer, Ovid, Hesiod, La Fontaigne and Apollonius,
Have been narrated in verse with attention to detail.
By the way, this author cooked up the King- Cook tale.

****

The King and the Cook

Many years ago, in Hindustan, there was a king,
And he was fond of grouching about everything.
He fumed if his subjects held their heads high;
He fretted when he found them too obsequious.
He lost his temper if they wore a solemn or wry
Face, or if they became too merry or hilarious.

Upright people filled him with embarrassment,
Dishonest rogues aroused his righteous anger,
Stupid people filled him with bitter resentment,
Wise people irked him, made him feel inferior,
Working people shocked him, offended his eyes,
He hated the stinking rich and cut them to size.
Obvious flattery he despised with all his heart.
He found the frank, outspoken people too smart.
He sincerely believed: a person who is powerful
Has no reason to be consistent and predictable.

Courtiers, guards and menials employed by him
To serve under him in different capacities daily
Found their position utterly vulnerable and grim
And were not able to perform their duties properly,
Not knowing when he'd be pleased to be displeased,
Or when the king should be displeased to be pleased.
They became overactive when they ought to be cool,
They acted shrewdly when they should play the fool;
Naturally, they were not able to rectify their faults,
For their careful actions produced opposite results.

The dire consequences of His Highness's vexation,
Occurrence of which defied all logical explanation,
Were flogging, beating, branding or incarceration
Or putting the offender to death by slow starvation.
The king devoted some time daily to deep thinking,
To devise ways to torture his victims before killing.
Sometimes the victim was forced to lay a wager
And to wrestle with a professional body-builder

Who would inevitably overpower him and take
Ten or twenty minutes to break the man's neck.
Sometimes the victim was given a pocketknife
To fight with a hungry tiger to save his own life.
The king believed that in the matters of justice,
There needn't be any room for mercy or leniency.

To our present-day readers it may appear surprising
That the people of that period tolerated such a king.
They should have risen en masse in an insurrection,
Or they should have resisted such autocratic action.
But the people of that era were rather superstitious
About their kings and entertained some odd notions.

They believed, although kings resembled other men,
They were really God's representatives from heaven;
That the world being so big and God being only one,
God's people take care of terrestrial administration;
That the king ruled until God finalized new selection;
That action against the king was considered treason.
Any disapproval of king's misdemeanor was impious;
To find fault with the king was outright blasphemous.
As God always transmitted His orders via the king,
Any refusal to obey the king's diktats was sinning.

The consequences of treason, blasphemy and sin
Were epidemics, flood, failure of crops and famine.
Hierarchies are divinely determined for every man,
Just as the planets are made to move round the sun.
Such ideas and beliefs dinned forcibly into the ears
Of ordinary citizens, made them cringe and cower,
Stuffed their innocent heads with apocryphal fears,
Which divinized the king and sanctified his power.

Only the old minister knew the king's vulnerability,
But he hid his knowledge under his turban of duty.
He knew a few drops of poison or a carving knife
Was more than sufficient to finish off a king's life.
But the king's death, he knew, won't be a solution,
For the universal belief in his heavenly connection

Would surely undermine his well-meaning action
And the law and order would take a ruinous course.
A bad king, he knew, was much better than chaos.

The wise minister was constantly tensed up inside,
But he always took care his internal tension to hide.
He tried to show his at-ease-ness by walking slowly;
His cheerfulness was showcased in a wooden smile.
He didn't know for what omission he'd be rewarded
And for what commission, he would forfeit his head.

Now a word about this king's divine appearance:
His narrow forehead crowned his pumpkin face;
His complexion was that of the un-burnt bricks;
His nose was sandwiched between his fat cheeks;
His eyebrows resembled a pair of fat caterpillars;
His moustache was a jumble of straggling wires;
His eloquent eyes glinted with perpetual unrest;
His goatee, like a cow's tuft, trickled to his chest;
He was a man of substantial bulk and good height;
His longish hair, lined with some strands of white,
Was parted in the middle, tended sideways in rows
And ended curled up exactly like an eagle's claws.
His royal nape was padded with lumps of blubber;
So the king was not able to hold his head straight,
But always glared like an ox straining at its tether.
He used to hobble along with a slow stooping gait.

In the spacious interior of the king's castle of skin
The Seven Deadly Sins roomed with kith and kin:
Pride, implacable lechery, envy, greed and wrath,
Covetousness, gluttony, drunkenness and sloth,
Casual cruelty, trickery, pettifoggery and caprice,
Hypocrisy, craftiness, readiness to lie and malice.
They bred like locusts, grew like tropical weeds;
He adored his tenants and catered to their needs.

This king despised to be called by any other name
But as the king of kings, for he thought it a shame

To be the king of a horde of such wretched humans
Who were even unworthy of being his garbage cans.
In fact, this 'king of kings' was only a feudal lord;
And his kingdom was rather small, which measured
One hundred by hundred fifty miles, or slightly more.
It could not extend any further, for it was peninsular.
Most of the landmass was covered with mountains,
Granite hills, sand beds, forests and bosky terrains,
Which were not suitable for grazing and cultivation.
So its population was about three and a half million.
Epidemics, natural calamities like drought and flood,
Evils like poverty, shabby conditions, malnutrition,

And this king's unquenchable thirst for human blood
Must have stemmed the further growth of population.

The king of kings, regarded as God's ambassador,
Was just another feudal tributary to the Emperor.
For that reason, he was given military protection
Against civil insurgency and external aggression.
The king, however, had a large retinue of hirelings,
Raised a gang of ruffians and a coterie of quislings;
And a squadron of bodyguards to protect his person,
And muzzle people capable of independent opinion.

The king had a group of advisers to compensate
For his lack of leisure and patience to deliberate.
He gave them full liberty to offer their opinions,
But he always reserved for himself the options
To apply his discretion and take final decisions
Without bothering about their legal implications.

So our so-called king of kings was riding
Roughshod over his submissive populace;
Whittling down their resistance, creeping
Like a malignant tumour, or a malfeasance;
Like a baobab in African forests, spreading
Out in all directions in relentless progression
Leaving no room for any vestige of vegetation.

Our king's seraglio was a supermarket of soft flesh
Where dolled-up beauties waited in pining readiness,
With passions marinated in the wine of anticipation
And baked in the furnace of deferred consummation.
It was an elegant ambience, a gourmet's dreamland.
It was a market where supply far exceeded demand.

In the seraglio lived twenty-seven young concubines;
A pampered lot, who loved to call themselves queens,
Guarded by many zombie-like eunuchs and manikins,
Recreated by a zany troupe of castrati and harlequins.

This king bristled with whims just as a porcupine
With darts; his temper was flighty as the weather,
And as inflammable as methane gas and gasoline.
He firmly believed nothing goes so well with power
As whim; that nothing so well becomes a great ruler
As moustache, sloth, eccentricity and contradiction.
But he trimmed his moustache, tempered his nature
With periodic fits of good humour and compassion.

Once His Majesty suffered from the common cold.
His leeches prescribed that a bath in human blood
Would prove an instantaneous and effective cure.
As it has been recorded by the palace chronicler,
The king's henchmen and butchers did a neat job
By filling, with human blood, a fairly big bathtub.
A bloodbath cured him of catarrh and snotty nose,
So he felt much indebted to those unknown heroes
Who'd sacrificed their lives for such a noble cause.
So he gave each of the sad families a princely sum
As a reward for their selfless and loyal martyrdom.

On one occasion, a Brahmin with his sacred thread
Aroused the king's pent-up anger, envy and hatred.
"You are flaunting your higher caste," the king said,
"Now, choose between your thread and your head."
The man preferred his thread and that irked the king.
He got him branded with hot iron instead of killing.

The man looked up and cursed: 'If my tears are true,
O evil king, your family will meet its end with you.'
The king was amused and said: 'This fellow is bold;
Give him five acres of land and thirty pieces of gold.'
His order was immediately carried out, and the man,
Walked tottering out of the court in great confusion.

The king shared family resemblances
With some notorious monsters of yore,
Who had been loosed upon the hapless
Humanity by the satanic forces of Nature.
They outraged the innocent, spilled blood
And caused havoc like epidemics or flood.

Our religious Scriptures and mythological tales
Supply us with some esoteric and wishful details:
That whenever a human or composite monster
Makes our good planet Earth sad and insecure
For us, God Himself or His son or His daughter
Or an archangel incarnates as a heroine or a hero,
And incensed by humankind's plight and sorrow,
Takes those death-dealing monsters by the horn,
Thus saving the human race from further attrition.

But our ordinary, practical experiences do tell us
That mankind need not depend on incarnations
All the time to rid itself of such cruel monsters.
Most often very canny and resourceful mortals,
By taking advantage of the monster's weakness
And using their natural cunning and confidence,

Play upon the caprices of their feared liege-lord,
Thereby hoisting the rogue with his own petard.

This king had an irresistible weakness for alcohol
And he generally preferred foreign brands to local.
He was both a dipsomaniac and a true connoisseur
Of the bottled mischief. So he maintained a cellar
Of all brands and that was always full to capacity.
Nine wine experts worked overtime to maintain it.

The king, as a rule, made his own selections
Of the brands to suit his moods and occasions.

When in the company of fun-loving women,
He relished the divine flavor of champagne.
He drank gin with mineral water when glum;
When worry and anxiety gave him migraine,
He mixed Bloody Mary with the priestly rum.
If he felt relaxed, he drank claret with honey;
After confronting a mirror, he guzzled martini.
If news pleased him, he spoilt himself with sack;
While meting out penalties, he asked for cognac.
When he was bored, he felt a temptation to cry;
So chose to pass out with whisky made from rye.
Before lunch he lashed his appetite with brandy,
A full bottle of brown sherry just before dinner;
If he was in a jovial mood or reasonably randy,
He tossed off vodka spiked with country liquor.
When thirsty, he, instead of drinking plain water,
Quaffed bottles of red wine and tankards of beer.

He preserved the vintage Scotland whisky
For the most demanding hour of the night,
That was, just before striding into his risky
Coliseum of love or the treasure-trove of delight
Where, trying to cope with an excess of desire,
He failed to perform owing to his fear of failure.

The king impressed the world as a virile man,
But in his seraglio, he was a flop, an also-ran.
He drooled over the eager bodies, he promised,
He fantasized; and he tried as much as he could.
He rushed his concubines like a fury, he aroused
Their passions, but alas, he was not at all good.
Such nocturnal embarrassments, we may aver,
Affected him, and he muddled along from day
To day; his mood was sour; his face was dour;
He looked constrained when he tried to be gay.

One late evening, the king was wining and dining,
The capacious dining table was full to the brim;
His minister, wearing a turban, was supervising
The victuals, appearing at once solemn and prim.
Suddenly the king rose and glared at the minister.
An implacable form of anger flashed through him,
Because, in the spiced belly of a full-roasted hare,
He found some colorful feathers of a woodpecker.
He had a feeling they were deliberately put there;
That convinced him that things had gone very far!

"You feeding me feathers, turban!" he bellowed,
Holding up a tiny feather for the minister to see.
The minister was visibly shaken and swallowed
His spittle and said hastily: "My lord, it is not me.
How could they be so careless? It is high treason.
I *think* that careless cook Naga Singh is to blame.
I *think* that cook Naga Singh has little or no reason
To be so inattentive. I *think* it is a matter of shame!"

"I am surprised," the king croaked, "you still *think*.
Don't you know it is just like poisoning my drink?"
"Yes," the minister mumbled, "it's worse than that.
Poison kills, but a feather would stick to the throat
And Your Highness would be forced to cough a lot.
It won't go in or come out, and give much discomfort."

"Shut up, you fool! I don't understand what you talk.
First bring the cook here quickly!" shouted the king.
And the cook was brought to him bound in padlock.
"Why on earth you feed your king feathers, Singh?"
The king rasped, but Naga was a tough nut to crack.

Six feet six, swarthy, handsome, young and clever
Quietly proud, self-assured and reasonably brave,
He heard the accusation and quickly thought over
How to defend himself and his poor head to save.
Hugely successful with cuisine and pretty women,
He loved his life. He did not want to die so young.

"My master, I never did it. What can I hope to gain
By putting feathers in the food? I know it is wrong.
Of one thing I'm pretty sure: There is a conspiracy
Against me, and this feather is a portion of that plot.
I've a hunch the person who had done it is a hussy;
Her name is Sipra, a maid, a most pernicious slut."

The king started up at these words, and fidgeted.
"Who you mean? Speak up!" he screamed at him.
With an ominous deliberation, he turned his head.
His brows furrowed menacingly; he let off steam.

"It's that scullery-woman Sipra," Naga Singh said:
"My Lord, she had threatened me to take my head.
That pesky stormy petrel creates a lot of problems
For all male workers there. She even calls us names.
The other day, I found her flaunting a precious gem;
I don't know if she steals, but she knows no shame.
She drags us into mischief, she ogles and wiggles,
She teases us, disturbs us, she swings her big hips,
She drops obscenities quite casually and she giggles
Impishly and, trying to provoke us, she even strips."

"Stop that nonsense, SHUT UP! You insolent man!"
The angry king barked out; he felt very deeply hurt.
"You pulled her hair today; you pinch her too often;
You whacked her buttocks. You must pay for that."

Naga winced, mortified by the king's omniscience.
It struck him as a proof of his heavenly connection.
Though somewhat scared, he tried to make his case
By shifting the blame to Sipra, that nebulous woman.
"Yes, my Lord," he said, "your accusations are true.
I have slapped her butt, and I have pinched her blue,
Because she's a law unto herself, a perfect Bedouin;
Though a mere maid, she carries herself as a queen.
She chews tobacco-laced betel and spits everywhere.
May the Devil take that scheming and villainous tart!
She'd secretly put these feathers in this roasted hare.
Though I'm innocent, I have to lose my head for that."

Naga Singh quite convincingly pleaded his case,
Thanks to his native courage and impromptu wit,
But he unknowingly erred; he could hardly guess
The gravity and the portentous outcome of his guilt.
Inadvertently, he hit the nest of hornets with a sling,
For Sipra had a romantic connection with the king.
She gave the king what his many queens could not:
They chilled his blood, but she could make him hot.

Though the king could have married her publicly
To regularize his romance, -and there was no one
Who had the courage to call his action unseemly-
He seemed to have felt a preternatural attraction
For a kind of relationship which was clandestine.
Keeping tryst increased the flow of his adrenalin.
Only on a wobbly bed, on a frayed carpet of guilt,
Besieged by the bedbugs of self-inflicted anxiety,
Sequestered by shame and turned on by secrecy,
The king was able to discover his truant potency.

"Off with his head!" the king gave his judgment,
"This arrant knave, I am sure, has lived too long;
This man is too guilty for any lesser punishment,
Because this rogue has done not just one wrong.
Feathering my food is no doubt a punishable act;
But molesting a woman is much worse than that."

Naga Singh, innocent, young, handsome and tall
Was forthwith led to the place where heads roll.
According to the custom, after about half an hour,
The minister brought a fresh sample of execution
To the king: a full cup of warm blood on a platter.
He felt relieved and heaved a sigh of satisfaction.

But the old minister looked very pale and sick.
Sweated profusely and trembled like an epileptic.

The king said: "Now that the chef is dead and gone,
You old turban, it is your first job to locate and bring

A new cook who should be a careful and polite man,
And can prepare better dishes than that Naga Singh."

The old minister as well as all other king's men
Found many reputed cooks for the royal kitchen:
Those cooks tried to cook as well as Naga Singh
And surprise, with cuisine, the palate of the king.
Three days passed, then five, then one full week,
And the king grew very disgusted, very dyspeptic.
Pastries and cakes were much harder than a brick,
His favourite pheasant soup reeked of raw garlic,
Curries were either very insipid, or spicy and hot,
Butter turtle meat smelled much like stale yogurt.
Kidney pudding and pancakes had no taste at all;
Grilled goat-meat and kebabs tasted like charcoal.

His nocturnal disappointments in the seraglio,
Now this tasteless food and his loss of appetite
Made him livid, pushed him into an imbroglio,
And his acute depression increased his brutality.

Once he thought aloud: "It was indeed a rash act
To kill such an able cook as Naga Singh like that.
I shouldn't have sent that insolent man to heaven
Where he must be performing his culinary wonders
To satisfy his new masters. Our loss was their gain.
That too for feathers! It was a blunder of blunders.
These new cooks, when they cook meat or biryani,
Why are they so different, why they taste so funny?"

Courtiers heard him, but had nothing more to say.
After all, it was he who sent the cook up, not they.

Once the king spoilt himself in a pre-dinner orgy;
Quaffed a crazy cocktail of whisky, rum and beer.
He got absolutely sozzled and his mind got fuzzy.
He was possessed with an intense feeling of power
And believed that everything was possible and easy.

"Bring Naga Singh here, quick, I give you two hours,"
He commanded his minister and trembling courtiers,
And added a rider: "If you fail to carry out my orders,
You will be horsewhipped, or I may cut off your ears."

"O my king of kings!" pleaded the horrified minister,
"It's an absolutely unrealistic impossible proposition.
You have sent that cook to heaven just for a feather.
He is dead and gone. Can we bring back a dead man?"
"Nothing doing!" the king said, "You heard my order.
Now it's your duty to produce him before my throne."

The old minister expressed his utter helplessness:
"Please, give me some more time. Your Highness
May be aware that heaven is such a distant place.
Our messengers and cavalrymen would have to go
There and come back. You know our men are slow.
Besides, the gods there may not be willing to spare
So readily such an excellent cook like Naga Singh.
In that case our earthly soldiers will declare a war
Against the gods of heaven, and only after defeating
Them, they can bring Naga Singh back to our king."

The king relented: "All right, I give you four hours.
If you fail to bring him, I'll first see your two ears
(He twitched the old man's ear) on a silver platter.
Then all our useless courtiers will part with theirs.
I wonder if your ears are cut off, you can still hear!"
He told his executioner to be ready with the shears.

Now, this narrator craves his readers' indulgence
To bear with him for having kept them in suspense.

Our unjustly condemned master cook Naga Singh,
Dressed as a housemaid, was living and cooking,
In absolute secrecy, in the minister's big building.
Transvestism as a camouflage has a long tradition.
Some great ancient heroes like Achilles and Arjuna,
For strategic reasons, wore the apparel of a woman
For some time, using it as a guise to evade detection.

The minister was undoubtedly a resourceful man,
For he anticipated trouble and could rightly guess,
While leading Naga Singh to the place of execution,
That, in future, such an occasion would come to pass.
He, however, based his guess on his own experience
Of king's vagaries caused by wine-induced madness.
He was able to take the executioner into confidence,
Advised him to spare the cook and slaughter a goat
And bring to him some freshly shed blood in a pot.
Then he led Naga Singh to a safe and secluded spot,
Gave him a set of woman's clothes he had brought
And instructed him to be dressed as a shy woman,
To pull the veil low in order to hide his moustache.
Clad in a sari, Naga Singh looked truly Amazonian
And was conducted cautiously to an unknown place.

Waiting for the cook's arrival in a drunken condition
Was really tiring. The king was bored and had a nap.
When he blinked open his eyes, he saw an apparition
Dressed in a milk-white overall and a white cloth-cap,
Blessing him with a cool smile, though condescending.
He took time to place a sartorially altered Naga Singh.
Our resurrected cook was all set on doing a thespian
In order to teach his bete noire the king a dire lesson.

But the old minister looked very pale and sick,
Sweated profusely and trembled like an epileptic.

"Where had you been all these days, Naga Singh?"
Quizzed the inebriated and utterly confused king,
 "It was our hasty decision, that we realized later.
We transferred you to heaven only for a feather."

"You did a handsome thing by me," the chef said,
"By ordering your executioner to cut off my head.
I openly admit that only through your good offices
I am living in much better personal circumstances.
You may have your own selfish reasons to rue,
But my life in heaven is just a dream come true.

I've permanently bidden farewell to mortal strife
And stress by dying, though prematurely, into life."

"What's that, Naga Singh? How can that be true?"
The king inquired: "Actually, I could not get you.
What type of life you dead people lead out there?
Is that heaven better than our terrestrial sphere?"

Naga Singh cleared his throat, smiled patiently;
He seemed to have learnt to tolerate human folly.
"This earth is to heaven is what a beggar is to you;
That is the equation," he said: "I thought you knew.
Heaven is what all people dream of, but do not get
Till they are killed by a king or court or in accident.
Or until, grown old, they eschew their mortal state,
Though the last mode of dying, I think, is quite late."

"Aha," the king said: "Naga Singh, you talk wisely!
It seems of late you've acquired some speaking skill.
Tell us briefly about that country's real plus points.
Do all people out there put on only white garments?
You needn't take offence, but it's my harmless frolic;
In this outfit, you really look like an elongated garlic."

Naga famously ignored the king's snide observation,
And continued his tale in a mood of total absorption:

"The combined efforts of a poet and a photographer,
O king, can give you an idea of heaven's atmosphere.
There the light breeze blows perfumed with romance;
Your Rati and Kandarpa are my next-door neighbors.
The streams flow smoothly with crystal-clear water;
The ground is carpeted all over with fragrant flowers.
The best thing about heaven is its moderate weather
Which is a sweet confluence of winter and summer.
Nights are not quite dark; days are not quite bright;
The sky glows lambently as in a springtime twilight.
As the moon is always full, both our days and nights
Are almost identical; your stars are our streetlights.

"During the daytime, the sunshine, passing through,
And lampshaded by, floating clouds, fluffy and blue,
Floods our heaven's landscape with a cozy shimmer.
That moderate weather gives us an equable nature.
There all types of flowers bloom, all the birds sing
And purple grapes grow in vines all the year round.
Citizens of heaven get everything just for the asking;
Golden horns of plenty lie unattended on the ground.
There's no idea of private wealth; so we don't hoard;
We have plenty of all things, yet we never get bored.

"In that dreamland, you earthlings call it paradise,
There's no disease, no old age, no insects or flies.
I was pleased to notice that the natives of heaven,
I mean the gods, freely socialize with us, the men
Who have achieved immortality simply by dying.
As we have nothing to lose, but everything to gain,
We spend our time by wining, dining and dancing.
Well, I feel like telling you, my one-time master,
That they have given me a castle of blue sapphire
To reside and thirty-one damsels for my pleasure."

The king was impatient and blurted out: "Hey, Naga,
About weather and availability, you're going ga ga.
Why don't you tell us about the quality of their wine,
Which is capable of making any damn place divine?
Do your gods there drink? Can they make a cocktail?
If not, your heaven, I tell you, is as bad a place as hell."

"Once there", said Naga, "You will not complain
About anything. Their wines have such a flavour.
Compared to which, your sherry and champagne
Would taste far worse than vinegar or soda water.
Compared to their alcoholic drinks, your dry gin,
Your Scotch whisky, brandy, toddy, rum and beer
Would taste like worm-wood or even horse urine.
So, you won't find a single god who is a non-taker."

"Say what?" exclaimed the utterly outraged king,
For he had never faced such a humiliation before.

For the first time he was embarrassed for having
Indulged himself with horse piss and soda water.
Besotted with a deliciously cooked-up paradise,
Feeling barmy, disgruntled and pissed as a newt,
The king moped around, and he began to despise
His world and himself; his fixation became acute.

"We hate this life!" he whimpered. "My good chef,
You take us there quickly (He meant only himself):
"We would have many times of what you have got,
Because you're just a cook, and we are a big shot.
If a mere cook is given there a castle of sapphire,
We have every reason to aspire for a big empire.
Woe is me, Naga Singh! If I had known it earlier
That the people we killed as a punitive measure
Or sometimes for our caprice or for our pleasure
Were transported physically to a posh elsewhere,
We might have decided to minimize such murder.
To be frank with you, Naga, we feel truly cheated
To have given such comforts to people we hated."

'Forget it,' Naga said: 'They will go there after all.
You can't hope of making your subjects immortal.
Human beings on this earth are perishable things;
Only when they perish, they become divine beings.'

The king stood up and lurched towards Naga Singh.
"I hope", he repeated, "You will oblige your ex-king!
You know our royal desire. So take us there quickly."
"How can I?" said Naga: "None can simultaneously
Live in both the worlds. I mean it. There is the rub!
That's why, in heaven, there is a popular proverb:
If we want omelettes, eggs we would have to break;
We have to open up our fists for a warm handshake.
Birds must spread out their wings if they want to fly
To partake of the felicities of heaven, men must die.
Can you eat a bird, if it is baked with all its innards?
Like that our gross bodies are detested by the gods."

"I see, I see!" the king said "I think I got you right.
We are all set to go at once, even this very night."
Then he leaned forward and confided in a whisper:
"We are interested to take with us our Sipra dear,
Because, I'm afraid, even in heaven, I'd miss her.
Again, tell me clearly if you'd cook for me there."
All the courtiers present could hear his whisper.

"You aren't very sensible, I see," said Naga Singh:
"Tell me, what's so special about that Sipra thing?
Of course, you may take with you any worldling
You want to; that's rather easy. But why bother?
There, you will have many chances to have affair
With plenty of doe-eyed damsels if you so desire.
Believe me, the maidservants there would surpass
Your prettiest concubines in physical appearance;
And that slattern Sipra will cut a very sorry figure
In the elitist company of heavenly damsels there.
Once there, you won't even bother to look at her.
You really love my cooking? That I never knew.
If you appoint me as a cook, I will cook for you."

The king was delighted and decided to go alone.
He was mentally prepared for his transmigration.
"Call in our executioner," thundered he, beaming
At his courtiers who looked timidly at each other.
"Give us a hearty send-off, let the choristers sing
To celebrate our journey to the Celestial Empire.
I die here only to live in heaven; I am raring to go!
Anybody who would try to hold me back is my foe."

His six hefty bodyguards were watching the show;
Some of them were stupid, but the rest could know
What was up. One of them, determined to intervene,
Went to the king and said: "My lord, you're taken in.
As far as I know, nobody comes back if he be dead."
But the king, annoyed at his impertinence, exploded:
"Mind you, if my trip to heaven is any more delayed,
Before I leave, I will get all men present here gelded."

All present there fixed their gazes on Naga Singh
(Whom some took to be a genuinely divine being).
But he stood looking unflappable in his white outfit.
The executioner swiped his shining axe at the king,
And, at a single stroke, the fat royal throat was slit.
His body stood erect while his head lay on the floor.
It was bloody sight, utterly incredible and macabre.

King's apotheosis was so unexpected and so sudden
That the minister and courtiers took time to recover
From their violent nightmare, from their stupefaction;
The atmosphere was electrified with a spooky terror.

Finally, they could manage to say this: "Oh my God!
I had never imagined our king had so much of blood."

Then Naga Singh cleared his throat and slowly said:
"My good lords, you have had enough of trembling.
The darkness is gone and you have nothing to dread.
Now, let's make our minister and my savior our king."

The royal court was full; all looked at the minister
And requested him with one voice to be the ruler.
But the minister smiled like one who knew better
And said: "Friends, you are again inviting danger.
In good earnest, I am telling you: it is hazardous
To entrust absolute power to such a timid jackass
Who has spent his entire life by running errands,
And bending over backwards to humour his boss.
Though a bit clever, I doubt my own ability to rule.
Absolute power, I know well, is a dangerous tool
Which should not be given to a slave-minded fool.
I know how to feel nervous while appearing cool.
A cretin who, with a grin, has digested humiliation
So long doesn't have self-esteem., and such a man,
As soon as he finds himself in a position of power
Will have no respect for others' dignity and honour.
Of course, I am not sure in my case, too, it'd be so;
But how power corrupts a person, you never know."

The minister's frank words naturally embarrassed
All courtiers. Then he continued his talk and said:
"From whatever I have known about Naga Singh,
He is dignified, resourceful, and every inch a king.
I gave him a role and the general outline of a tale,
I'd never imagined that he would act it out so well.
Just imagine my fate had he slipped up on detail!
I advised him to oblige the king by cooking for him,
But enticing the king to kill himself was his scheme.
If the other world were half as good as his narration,
To continue in this world must be a real deprivation.
Believe me friends, I am not in the least exaggerating,
While listening to him I'd an urge to follow the king.
Now let our risen angel slip into the role of our king.
Give him a loud ovation, and let our choristers sing."

All people there clapped and shouted in one voice:
Naga Singh is our king. Naga Singh is our choice.

All were silent for a while. Then an ancient courtier
Knitted his hoary brows and put a sudden damper:
"Wait a bit. We all agree that Naga is a clever man.
But is it enough to make him worthy of the throne?
When we are entrusting our country and our future
To him, shouldn't we want to know his character?
I'll put him to a test, and if he rises to the occasion,
I'll have no objection to his ascending to the throne.
Now, Mr. Singh, tell us what is the very first thing
You'll do if we finally decide to make you our king?"

"The first thing, grand dad, I'd do is to rush to bed."
Then he remembered something, and said: "Oh, no!
I am moved really to see you so tense and depleted.
All of you are quite famished, your faces tell me so.
I should replenish your stomachs before I let you go.
Here are my first orders, you wouldn't go home until
I give all of you a practical proof of my culinary skill.
If you remember, it was the skill that brought me here
And saved all of us from the tentacles of that monster.

Once you select me as your king, I shall be your host;
So, as long as I am in the kitchen, wait here you must."

The ancient asker, wisest of them all, beamed a smile,
And said: "You'll make a good king, that too in style."

Other courtiers looked askance at the ancient courtier,
For they couldn't make out the question and its answer.
He said: "Most rulers do what's only expected of them.
By so doing and by following all the rules of the game,
They play a dull game and somehow manage the show.
They want to be praised for maintaining the status quo.
But the rulers who do more than they're expected to do
By eschewing conventions, by breaking a code or two,
By being innovative, by flying more and fluttering less,
They are the men who succeed in making a difference.
In such original rulers, power doesn't go to their head;
Each artisan is their friend; each soldier their comrade.
Power, for them, is an opportunity to be actively useful;
So instead of being arrogant, they become very humble.
As you know, it is not according to the rule of the book
That people should quiz a king, and a king should cook
Food to feed his subjects and bother about their hunger.
Now, we wish to be ruled by such a king with pleasure."

First the minister clapped his hands in full approval
Of what the courtier said; then he was joined by all.
"Let's do," he said, "a little more than expected of us.
Our king has set an example; let's emulate our boss."

The minister held aloft the crown now dripping red
And placed it reverentially on Naga Singh's head.
Naga Singh had to submit to the popular mandate
With a solemn attitude, for it was a decree of Fate.
Then he said: "Henceforth, rich or poor, every one
Must hold their own heads as upright as they can.
Our kingdom has become a wound of the universe,
Which can only be healed by our collective efforts.
I shall not relax, my courtiers, you take it from me,

Till I improve its condition, and make all of you free
From poverty, from fear, from the necessity to flatter
A king to get what you deserve, say, food and shelter.
God Almighty has given us this fleeting life as a gift.
Let's be worthy of His gift. Let's live it. Let's love it.
I've told you everything I know; what more can I say?
Chill out and gossip when the cooking is underway."

****

The Cyclopes and Odysseus

As the Greek cosmogonists of yore inform us,
The birth of the Universe began with the Chaos.
Out of the Chaos were born Gaeae and Uranus.
In that chaotic world, the laws were rather lax,
So, Gaeae, the Earth married the sky, Uranus.
(In modern sense, their union was incestuous!)
Together, they begot the Cyclopes and Titans
And some ugly-looking and huge Hecatonchires.

Uranus, peeved about his children's appearance,
Stowed away those Hecatonchires and Cyclopes
Into the Tartarus and ate up a number of Titans
As soon as they were born. He, alas, didn't bother
To know how his brutality would pain the mother.
The earth mother Gaeae was predictably outraged
To see helplessly her begotten children so savaged.
So, she conspired with Cronus, her youngest son,
To enfeeble Uranus through sexual emasculation,
Thereby teaching her uncaring husband a lesson

Once when Uranus was getting on bed with Gaeae,
Cronus cut off his manhood and threw it into the sea.

Then Cronus married his sister Rhea, and liberated
His siblings, Titans and Hecatonchires, from captivity.
But he did not liberate the Cyclopes, for he also hated
Them just like his father, for their physical deformity.
They lived happily till Rhea discovered to her horror,
That Cronus, in brutality, was no better than his father.
Fearing lest his children should surpass him in power,
He gobbled them up whole as a preventive measure.
It is, however, difficult to obtain figures by guesswork
About the width of his gullet or the size of his stomach.

Rhea sought the help of Gaeae who could understand
How painful it was to have a child-devouring husband.
Led by Gaeae, she took her son Zeus to Crete and hid
Him in Mt. Ida. There, Zeus grew up and made his bid
For authority, and removed his father from the throne
And forced him to vomit up his five babies one by one.
The children who were disgorged by Cronus his father:
Were Hestia, Hades, Poseidon, Hera and Demeter.
Thus began the rule of Zeus and other Olympians.
Then Zeus liberated the Cyclopes from the Tartarus.

Cyclopes Polyphemus

The Cyclopes were creatures of great size and might,
And known for the placement of their sense of sight.
Each Cyclops had only one eye, large, round and red,
And was horizontally fixed in the centre of his forehead.
Vulcan, the divine blacksmith, the limping god of fire
Liked them and made good use of their unique power.
When he was at his big furnace, fashioning hardware,
One of the Cyclopes helped him make the bellows roar,
And another would deal mighty strokes with a hammer.

The job of using the hammer needed full concentration
That the Cyclopes achieved with their undivided vision.

In course of time, their tribe grew and disintegrated,
And settled in different places. One group migrated
To the south-western coast of Sicily and did settle
There, with their flocks of sheep and herds of cattle.
They lived in caves and got used to rustic existence.
They were omnivorous, lacking in human kindness.
Like a mob of gigantic devils broken loose from hell
They killed and ate any animal or man they did spy
And they were able to spy distant things very well
Due to their big height and the location of their eye.

One horde settled in an island in the Mediterranean
And tended live-stock and stayed in the subterranean
Caves. The leader of the tribe was named Polyphemus,
The son of Poseidon and a female Cyclops Amphitrite.
Like the rest of his tribe, he used to graze his animals
All day long and herd them into his cavern at twilight.

One evening he returned as usual, and, to his pleasure,
He saw some eatable men loitering near his cave-door.
"I'm hungry! What a treat!" he said in a good humour.
Then he ate up one and singled out another for supper.

It's high time we told you something about Odysseus
Who could make good his escape from Polyphemus.

Of all the Greek potentates who sailed to Troy,
Fought for ten years and brought about its fall,
Odysseus was not only the wisest and wiliest guy,
But also was one of the bravest heroes of them all.
He drew a wrestling match with huge-limbed Ajax
And also beat him at a sprint in the friendly sports.
Adjudged the best, he received the arms of Achilles.
He was a rare hero who, like Hercules and Theseus,
By his physical prowess, could overpower Cerberus.
He entered the Hades to consult prophet Tieresias
About the nature of events that would come to pass.

Circe kept him for one year; Calypso for seven years
And finally she released him at the command of Zeus.
Great misfortunes he suffered in the hand of Poseidon.
The cause of Poseidon's anger will be shortly known.
Though some lesser scribes have maligned Odysseus
By calling him a shrewd conjuror of words and a fox,
He was a favourite of Pallas Athena and Shakespeare.
Poet Homer devoted an epic to the journey of this hero.
One of the finest novelists of modern era, James Joyce,
Saw a symbolic message in Ulysses' homeward voyage.
He was down innumerable times, but he was never out;
Though he played a couple of tricks, he was ever devout.
He lived his life and carried it off earnestly and famously.
As friends or as sworn foes, the gods took him seriously.

After sacking Troy, the kings who had joined their force
With king Agamemnon and Helen's husband Menelaus,
Collected the survivors of their troop, captives and loot
And headed towards home by sea, or by the land route.
Odysseus and his men set their sails and pulled the oars;
They were homesick and eager to see the Ithacan shores.
After ten years of separation, he nurtured just one hope:
To be reunited with son Telemachus and wife Penelope.

While voyaging, they found their provisions run down;
So they were forced to pillage Ismarus, a coastal town,
But spared Apollo's temple. So priest Maron sent a fine
Gift to them: twelve jars full of fragrant vintage wine.
Anon they encountered a sea-storm; tried to withstand,
But couldn't; their old ships were driven helter-skelter.
One morning, the sailors chanced upon a virgin island.
They cast anchors quickly and camped on the shore.
The inhabitants of that land were called lotus-eaters.
The lotus fruits they ate turned them into dreamers.
The unsuspecting sailors who strayed into that place,
Found there that fruit; it was available in abundance.
Then they gorged on that fruit, and that did the magic.
Its impact on the eaters' psyche was hallucinogenic.
Once they ate it, they began to laze, forgot their duty,

Recoiled from all types of activity; attained tranquility.
They were possessed with a feeling of buoyant elation,
A sense of perfect well-being, a feather-soft lassitude,
A quiet and cosy withdrawal, a total self-absorption,
And an all's-well-with-the-world -don't-worry attitude.

Previously some old sailors had forewarned Odysseus
To keep away from the magic land of the lotus-eaters.
By the time he realized that he had committed an error
By allowing his sailors to cast anchor near that shore,
It was already too late. Odysseus could see helplessly
Some of his sailors gorging on that lotus fruit greedily.

He ran to them and shouted his warning: "O comrades,
This land of the lotus-eaters is far worse than the Hades.
In the name of Athena, don't eat those dangerous fruits!
They'll make you forget your nature, mission and roots."

But the sailors who had already helped themselves on
The lotus fruit were already in the grip of hallucination.
They guffawed heartily as if Odysseus cracked a joke.
"Old chap," they said: "Leave us alone. We are in luck.
This missions and roots stuff is baloney and baby talk.
We're living in the best of all possible worlds; we lack
 Nothing in this place; nor do we want anything more.
Now, boss, please eat this fruit and forget your care."
Odysseus was not amused. He got them all hauled up
To their ships and secured them to the masts with rope.

After voyaging several months on the vast azure seas,
They sighted an island covered with lush green trees.
They thought it proper to make a brief stopover there
To collect food and furnish their pots with fresh water.
Odysseus picked up twelve men and set off to explore
The strange island and to locate a fountain or a boar.
They moved deep into the island, didn't meet a man,
But saw a clearing in front of a subterranean cavern.
Inside that cave they saw kids and lambs newly born,
Huge baskets of dry meat and chunks of goat cheese,
And they quickly helped themselves with great relish.

They wondered who could be the owner of that place.
They hoped to meet a shepherd and his shepherdess.

By and by, twilight deepened, and they could hear
The roar of some animal that sounded like thunder,
And the bleating and bellowing of sheep and kine.
Then they saw a giant herding animals coming near.
He was a massive primate holding an uprooted pine.
Some drew their swords, primed for a confrontation,
But Odysseus advised: "We can't beat this apparition.
Look here, he can easily trample down a full battalion.
Let's know whether he is a friendly or hostile person."

Polyphemus drew near his cavern and was amused
To find those humans, and said: "That's just dandy!"
He picked up one of them, a hefty one, and chewed
Him up, as a boy eats a stick of puffed cotton candy.
Then he picked up the stoutest sailor from the group
And said darkly: "Ha, his flanks will make a fine soup
And his brains a fine dessert. Truly, I am not a glutton.
As I haven't had human meat for long, I ate up that one.
Once in a blue moon I get humans. So I'll take no more
Than one at a time. You eat my cheese, get fat, feel free
And wait your turn. But never try to run away from here.
If you do, I warn you, men, none will be worse than me.
If you irk me, I shall go back on my present decisions."
Then he roughly shoved Odysseus and his companions
Into a narrow-mouthed cavern along with his live-stock
And closed the cavern's door with a big and heavy rock.

The light in the interior of that cavern was rather dim.
As the giant lay down to sleep, Odysseus went to him
And said politely: "Friend, after tending sheep and kine
You must be tired. Would you like to drink some wine?
A priest of Apollo has given us this jar of wine as a gift.
We would not mind at all if you drink up the whole of it."
The Cyclops peered at the man, couldn't see him clearly;
But he liked his suggestion and thanked him profusely.
"I am Polyphemus," he said: "What's thy name, buddy?"

"I am a Thessalian by birth, " said Odysseus, amicably:
"I am a mariner by profession, and my name is Nobody."

Polyphemus drank the whole jar of fragrant red wine,
Felt well-disposed to Nobody, and said: "You're a fine
Person. I killed your mate; still, you behave as a friend;
So, I'll return your good offices by eating you at the end.
By Poseidon, Nobody, I've never heard a name like that.

Odysseus

You look quite well-made, but, alas, you are not very fat.
If you like, you accompany me tomorrow to the pasture
Where I graze my animals. Milk will make you stouter."
Then he wolfed down one more of Odysseus's fellows,
Fell fast asleep, and soon started snoring like a bellows.

Odysseus made a campfire in one corner of the cave;
He was determined to take a great risk in order to save
Himself and his fellows. He heated his sword in the fire
And gouged out the single eye of the sleeping monster.
The blinded Cyclops howled loudly and groped around
And hollered: "Nobody has blinded me! Nobody is here!"

Some Cyclopes came near the cave hearing his sound;
But when they made out clearly what he was shouting,
They felt relieved and thought Polyphemus was joking:
"If nobody blinded him, why on earth is he hollering?"

The cave was spacious, crowded with sheep and cows;
To catch his enemies he had to scour about and grope-
Sozzled, maddened with pain- to get even with his foes.
But his foes kept dodging him, playing blind man's buff.
He could not catch his foes, and so became very glum,
And thought: "I trusted Nobody, and this is the outcome.
The rogue enticed me into drink, and I called him buddy!
And then he betrayed me; I must catch hold of Nobody."
He vowed not to trust again that sly creature called man.
What a terrible price he had to pay to learn this lesson!

In the morning, Polyphemus hit upon a workable plan:
To destroy his mutilators through thirst and starvation.
He stood astride at the cave's entrance and tried to feel
All animals with his hands, so that the men did not steal
Out of the cave and escape. Resourceful Odysseus gave
Advice to his men to hang on to sheep's bellies to save
Their life. He himself hung on to a sheep by holding on
To its wool and with trepidation, came out of the cavern.

One after another, all his sheep and cows came out.
Though unable to see, Polyphemus was able to count
His animals. He plugged the cave-door with that rock.
Then he realized that he could no longer tend his flock,
As he had already lost his most useful organ, his eye.
He couldn't know what to do, and felt a desire to cry.

But instead of crying, he wanted to vent out his anger
And, standing near the cave-door, he began to roar:
"Hey Nobody, O Thessalian punks, you disabled me,
Now no power on earth or in heaven can set you free.
I'll be avenged. I'll spend many nights under the sky.
Inside the cave, hungry and thirsty, you'll slowly die.
You may not live that long. I may call a friend or two
Who'll do to you, rogues, what I'm now unable to do. "

Odysseus heard his threats, and he felt really sorry
For the giant, for having reduced him to such misery.
When in a perilous situation, he had to come out of it
Either by dint of his courage and ability, or by deceit.
Calamity averted, he and his companions noiselessly
Walked to their anchored fleet and sailed immediately.
When Odysseus knew that he was at a safe distance,
He loudly and vainly declared himself to Polyphemus:
"O Polyphemus, we cheated you out of your pleasure
To feast on us or make us perish in thirst and hunger."

That was a piece of blustering, but to no purpose;
It only invited disasters, and made matters worse.
Those words further enraged the blinded monster,
And he grabbled for, found and held a big boulder
And, with full force, hurled it at the hated speaker.
Fortunately it missed Odysseus's ship by a whisker.

Again defeated, the giant invoked his sire Poseidon
And asked him to avenge his son's unjust mutilation.
Poseidon heard his prayer and set many an obstacle
For Odysseus and his men; he was worn to a frazzle.
Besieged by calamities, he lost his ships, his sailors
In the course of his journey that lasted full ten years.
Finally, dispossessed, drained off, dressed in tatters,
But still undaunted, he arrived at the Ithacan shores.

****

The Sirens and Orpheus

Entomologists working on spiders inform us
That there exist certain categories of spiders
In which females devour their male partners
After the mating. The female folk of Lemnos,
We are told, killed all their males in cold blood
To usher in a conflict-free and feminine world.
Now, these Siren sisters used their feminine guile
To attract sailors and devoured them with a smile.
The situation is both frightening and macabre!
Though they were good singers with long hair,
Those Siren sisters were not ordinary women,
For they had wings which enabled then to soar;
Like mermaids, they were able to live in ocean.

A Siren with a sailor

It was not possible for us to know for sure,
In that group, how many Sirens there were.
Some put the number at ten, some at four,
Some maintain that they were only seven.
There is no real need to fuss about a number.
The fact is that they were pernicious women
Who sang sweetly and played well on lyres,
Floating in the sky or standing on the shores.
Their target audiences were the lovesick sailors.
Their aim was to fire them with amorous desire,
So that they'd walk into their enchanted parlour.
When they saw the Sirens, they'd tarry a while
To listen to their mellifluous songs a little more.
Excited by their beauty, unaware of their guile,
Like sleepwalkers they would walk, one by one,
Through the flowery arbours to a shaded lawn,
To a velvety quilted carpet strewn with flowers
And plonk themselves down by the wily singers.

The Sirens sang to make their expectations soar
Till they completely had the men in their power;
Then they would, quite suddenly, stop singing,
Pounce on the unsuspecting lovers, and wring
Their necks and devour them with their talons
As the savages break and eat the water melons,
Until nothing was left off their unfortunate prey
Except for their skins, bones and beards gray.

Nothing tender moved those deceptive Sirens.
They used their noble gift for music as the bait
To lure and kill men who cried: "Oh, spare us,
We want to go home, to our dear ones who wait
For us. We love you; why are you so full of hate?"
But those Sirens ignored their pleadings and ate
Them up with more speed and greater satisfaction.
Pathetic cries of the sailors increased their appetite.
Theirs was a sad case (it will fill us with revulsion)
Of talent without a touch of nature, but full of spite,
Of beauty devoid of love, of hearts void of emotion.

Aphrodite, Zeus's daughter and the wife of Vulcan,
Is the goddess of love and promoter of procreation.
She despised those women for their inability to love,
And for that reason, she changed them into a drove
Of monsters with the wings and talons of vultures.
Their bodies changed in keeping with their natures.
She also cursed them: "If and when you encounter
A better musician, you'll lose your seductive power."

They were, however, allowed to keep their tresses,
Their physical features, their good voice and faces.
That's to say, they still had enough feminine charm
To captivate males and conceal their ability to harm.
Considering men's tendency to gloat, and to go nuts,
Over women's beauty and sidelong glances of tarts,
With only a fraction of the possessions they still had
The situation, perhaps, could have been equally bad.

Aphrodite

Some may say, that too with condign justification,
That only the weaklings easily fall for temptation.
So, they're destroyed owing to their own defects,
Say, like the flies blundering into a spider's nets,
Like the restless winged insects flirting with fire.
Man must atone for his acts of folly and his error

Of judgment. They heave a sigh of relief, and say,
Thank God, we won't face such dangers, any way.

But when the means of temptation seems aesthetic
The condition of a reasonable man is also pathetic.
Of all the wise heroes Ancient Greece has given us
None was wiser and more judicious than Odysseus;

Yet he felt tempted, though he was given instructions
By his old flame Circe to beware of the Siren sisters.

After the fall of Troy, Odysseus, in his remaining fleet
Sailed for his home island; and on his way he did meet
With many ordeals; one was his sojourn with the Circe.
(Homer narrates this incident in his epic, The Odyssey.)
Circe was an enchantress, no less cruel than the Sirens.
But instead of killing men, she turned them into stones
Or beasts. That she spared Odysseus did clearly prove
That, though cruel, she had a heart responsive to love.
When her lover prepared to leave her after a year or so,
She said ruefully: "O Odysseus, you know I let you go
Against my desire, with a heavy heart and great grief.
For which woman wouldn't wish to permanently keep
The man she loves so much? Who'd want separation
After tasting the celestial pleasures of physical union?
But I'm afraid, if you do not take sufficient precaution,
The Sirens will tempt you and destroy to the last man."

For her kind words and valuable information,
Odysseus thanked her profusely and sailed on.
With wax, he sealed the ears of his companions,
For, he feared that they had no such self-control
As he himself had to resist the Sirens' temptations

Even after knowing well that they were quite fatal.
He wanted to enjoy the Sirens' songs just the same
And defeat those fatal songsters in their own game.
"Be assured, chaps," he bragged, "you wait and see:
Their magic, their good looks will be wasted on me."
But his companions had had enough of distress,
So they did not want to take any more chances,
And tied Odysseus to the ship's mast with cordage.
He was vastly amused and yielded to his bondage
With an amused smile. He knew that their anxiety
Was caused by their love for him and for his safety.
He cocked up his ears and waited with anticipation
To see the Sirens and enjoy their musical rendition.

By and by, that enchanted island hove into view.
They thrilled to bits to experience something new.
Soon, they saw some pretty damsels on the shore,
And some of them were hovering gently in the air.
An erotic scent was wafted to them from their hair.
Casting soft glances, they sang with a soft cadence
Of what had happened, what was about to take place.
They sang of the creation, of the Titans and the Giants,
Of the dodos, of the ratites as heavy as the elephants,
Of mighty Olympians, of monsters, of winged horses,
Of the love-links of humans with gods and goddesses,
Of the exploits of the heroes, of the deeds of Hercules,
Of Odysseus in particular and his heroic feats in Troy,
Of passion of Apollo for Hyacinthus the charming boy.

"Come to us Odysseus, take your share of pleasure.
We know things; we celebrate only glory and valour.
Whatever you have heard about us is mere hogwash;
Tell us truly, do we really look so bad, so dangerous?
People call us temptresses; they do us great wrong;
We only bestow on you men our sweetness and song.
Women hate us so much because we are so lovable;
Men try to avoid us because they find us irresistible.
If you love our music, say, who or what prevents you
From coming to us, and spending here an hour or two?

For the joys of love, no warhorse baulks at a hurdle.
Love's delight, like the camel's milk, doesn't curdle."

Odysseus strove and wriggled like a trapped tiger
To set himself free, and to swim alone to the shore.
He bellowed, he pleaded, he threatened, he swore:
"Remove these ropes, you guys! This is my order."
Finally, he had to give up out of sheer indignation,
As his words, on his "deaf" men, had no impression.
They saw his spasmodic movements and pouting lips.
Like a tethered animal, he was straining at the leash.
An elderly man said: "Don't be so restive, Odysseus,
It is a temporary bout of infatuation, it will surely pass
As soon as we cross this island, and the Sirens stop
Their song. Remember your Penelope and cheer up.
If not old Penelope, think of your son Telemachus."

Odysseus barked at him like the hell-dog Cerberus;
Sent him to hell and threatened to drub him soundly
For such impertinence. He swore to cut off his head.

But the old sailor thus threatened smiled innocently,
Because he was unable to hear what Odysseus said.

Odysseus and his men could see as they passed by
Mouldering and fresh human bones banked up high
On the green turf of the island, a grim and benighted
Testimony of human weakness for music and beauty

And the subtle ferocity of the Sirens who delighted
In carrying on their slaughter with artistic ingenuity.

Those Sirens might have carried on their carnage
Unabated for quite some time, may be to our age,
Heaping bone on bone till those heaps did surpass
In volume and size (in colour too) Mount Olympus,
Had they not met their match (also their bete noire)
In a worthy youth from Thrace with the magic lyre.

His name was Orpheus, a name to conjure with,
Celebrated in poetry, folklores and many a myth.
Muse Calliope was his mother, Oeagrus, his sire.
He was a darling of Apollo who gifted him a lyre.

He was a great musician who did fantastic things
And moved the hearts of gods, men and the kings.
When he struck a note cyclones blew like a breeze;
Choppy seas stood still and hot tempers did freeze.
To revive his wife Eurydice, he entered the Hades
And charmed with his music Pluto and the shades.
Ferryman Charon, charmed by his song's power,
Readily ferried him across Styx, the Hades' river.
The enchanted Cerberus didn't stop him at the gate.
The tormentors of sinners suspended their torment;
For sometime, that continent of suffering and gloom
Was changed into a place of joy and began to bloom
Like a garden in spring. Ancient shades blessed him
For bringing sunshine to a world so dismal and dim.

[Three other heroes - Theseus, Odysseus and Hercules -
Had entered the Land of Death while still in the flesh.]

When Jason called upon the brave youths of Greece
To sail to Colchis with him to fetch the Golden Fleece,
Orpheus joined him carrying a lyre instead of a sword.
"Adventure with a lyre?" mocked Argonauts on board.
But he soon proved his power when the big ship Argo
Did not budge an inch from where it stood on the beach
Though all the Argonauts applied their full force to tow.
Orpheus strummed the strings, and lo, it began to hitch.
As the ship slid down into the waters of the Aegean Sea,
"Bravo!" exclaimed Jason, and the heroes danced in glee.

When storms raged and tidal waves howled like mad
Rising high and tossing the big ship like a plaything,
Brave hearts missed a beat and jolly hearts grew sad,
Orpheus sang a soothing song and plucked the string.
He played a tune that smoothed the sea's ruffled mien,

Storm clouds dispersed; the angry nature became kind,
The sailors exulted; their eyes sparkled like champagne.
And the big ship scudded merrily along before the wind.

He played on his lyre when drunken sailors brawled,
When winds didn't blow, when the sailors got bored,
When the tired rowers relaxed their hold on the oars,
When they grew home sick and longed for the shores.

One incident concerning a romantic confrontation
Took place on the deck. It truly deserves a mention.
Beautiful Atalanta, the solitary woman present there,
With a sailor's outfit, her fine figure and auburn hair
Tied in a simple knot, her splendid bow and quiver,
Her raffish charm, her demeanour austere and shy,
And, above all, her fame for not yet having a lover
Smote the male hearts and made passions run high.
One said cavalierly: "Mates, if any of you dare deny
That Atalanta is the loveliest woman under the sun,
 I may feel offended, and fight a duel with that man."

The youth wanted to please the lady by his chivalry;
Some were amused; some considered it an effrontery.
But Atalanta bristled with rage; for she did not like it.
She despised to be treated as an object of male vanity.
She reared herself up like a cobra and hissed in anger:
"You call me lovely? Damn it, you flatter me in vain,
I challenge you to a duel for treating me as a wager.
By holy Artemis, such insinuating rubbish I disdain."

The Argonauts knew in archery she had few rivals.
She had already killed Ares' boar and two Centaurs.
So they tried to placate her, but she waxed angrier
When her offended and brutally spurned admirer
Called her a frigid drag queen dressed as a sailor.
They were all set for a duel, all persuasions failed.
It became certain that one of them would be killed.
Orpheus was lazing when he was asked to interpose.
 He obliged and played a soothing passionate number.

The thorn became a bud, and the bud became a rose.
Atalanta flashed a sunny smile and forgot her anger.

Of all the great feats of Orpheus none was so lasting
And as beneficial to humanity as his Sirens-bashing.
The Argonauts knew nothing of those coy temptresses.
That apart, they were young, avid for new experiences.
They saw the pretty winged damsels singing sweetly.
The strangeness of the scene escaped them completely.
Adults, when they are crazed with the two intoxicants –
Curiosity and pleasure – they behave much like infants.

They beached the ship, rushed to the Sirens' snare,
Bopping just like the lemmings racing toward water,
Like mackerels they swam briskly towards the shore.
Fascinated by their seductive tone and their beauty.
What pleased them most was their easy availability.

Orpheus also felt the pull of desire to join the march,
But his second sight forced him to stay put and watch.
He saw piles of bones, but couldn't guess their imports,
Felt confused, smelt mischief, and told the Argonauts:
"Friends, your noble mission will be surely hamstrung
If you exchange or forget the Golden Fleece for a song.
Besides, if the things you long for are easily available,
They may be deceptive traps; to avoid them is advisable."
They didn't heed his warning. So he deemed it proper
To wean them away from Sirens by playing his lyre.
With his nimble fingers, he struck a melodious note.
He played this time with extra-care, for he knew a lot
Depended upon his scoring a victory over the Sirens,
As his companions were his country's famous scions.
He found Jason and his mates, like a load of morons,
Swooning over those suspicious-looking songsters.
Atalanta liked the music; and she could understand
Why her journey mates were making for the island.
These men, she mused sadly, are incorrigible sots;
At the very sight of pretty women, they are all nuts.

His music rose to a crescendo, and it filled the air;
It drowned the Sirens' song and stole their thunder.
The melodies the Sirens sang pampered the senses;
They were intended to stoke passions and to enthrall;
But the music Orpheus produced, its divine cadences,
Expanded the mind, calmed passions, exalted the soul.

Finally, the pernicious spell of the Sirens was broken.
The enchanted Argonauts emerged from their trance
Demystified, as if from a deep sleep they had woken
Up to another reality, wondered and looked askance
At each other. They realized their folly and got a grip
On themselves and finally they returned to their ship.

This version of the ancient anecdote has it so:
That the Argonauts had alighted from the Argo
And flocked to the Sirens' flower-strewn carpet
But made good their escape before it was too late.
There is another version, which runs as follows:
That they heard the Sirens' song while on board
And were raring to go to the shore when Orpheus,
Intending to save them, touched the right chord
With: "Comrades, let the Sirens sing as they may;
I can play on my lyre as well; let me give it a try."

He gave an impromptu performance on his lyre.
The Sirens yielded to Orpheus's superior power.
The Nereids of the sea hailed him as the winner.
His mates, for sometime, were in a double bind;
Finally, they sailed on leaving the Sirens behind.

The Sirens were afflicted with a severe depression
And looked utterly wretched and were crest-fallen.
Their musical and physical charms were lost upon
The sailors. They had never been beaten by any one
In music. So, they were a sort of addicted to victory.
When defeated, they lost their mystique, their glory,
As well as their wily ability to seduce and to enthrall.
To top it all, they also lost the means of their survival.

They lost their joy of life; their song became a groan;
In course of time, they were transmogrified into stone.

Do those good-looking and insidious-voiced Sirens
Leave any symbolic message to warn and edify us?
Maybe, yes: A thing or a person that captivates us
At first sight often turns out to be very pernicious.
Second, so sublime a thing as music can be a snare
To catch music lovers unawares and cost them dear.

Though Orpheus enthralled the world by his music,
Taken as a whole, his eventful life was truly tragic.
He married Eurydice, the woman he loved so well;
He was at the peak of his bliss when bad luck fell.
Lovely Eurydice was bitten by a venomous snake
And died instantly. Orpheus's poor heart did break.

Overcome with grief, he descended into the Hades
And demanded his wife be restored to him at once.
The king of the underworld Pluto granted his wish
And permitted him to take back his wife Eurydice
With one condition: that he must not turn around
In order to ascertain till he left the Hades' ground,
And if he did, he would lose his Eurydice forever.
But he looked back and she vanished into thin air.
That condition appeared innocuous, but it was not.
Man is a curious animal and curiosity kills the cat.
Unhappy Orpheus erred; but he was bound to err,
As he used his power to reverse the law of Nature.

His loving nature, his beauty and his musical genius
Couldn't protect him from the maenads of Bacchus.
To be true to the woman he loved, was Apollonian;
But it was against the spirit of Dionysian celebration.
Those ferocious maenads murdered him out of hate,
As he spurned their wild orgies and was Apollo's pet.
His severed head, still singing sadly, drifted to Lesbos
Where it prophesied accurately for several years,
And in course of time, he was given a divine status.
****

The Sleepless Dragon and Jason

Of all the familiar monsters that keep visiting
The human mindscape as fancy red herrings,
The dragons are probably the most enduring.
Sometimes as the harbingers of good things,
Sometimes as the abettors of actions evil,
Sometimes as vigilant and caring godlings,
Sometimes as the accomplices of the Devil
They've been traveling from nation to nation
Inspiring general interest, poetic imagination.

A Chinese Dragon

Some monsters like the Sphinx are only one,
Some like the Sirens have a countable clan,
But the number of dragon types is a legion.
They may be chthonic, aquatic, amphibious,
Sometimes like Jurassic birds they can fly.
Though some call them immortal creatures,
In certain mythical stories we see them die.

As human beings acquire different features
Like the Africs, Mongoloids and Caucasians,
The dragons of different climates and cultures

Have their separate physiognomic variations.
Their differences notwithstanding, it is clear,
They have certain physical aspects in common:

They have scaly bodies; they breathe out fire;
And have magical powers and are often reptilian.

Just imagine a lizard as long as a crocodile,
And a crocodile as tall as an African tusker
With a bat's wings and the head of a reptile
With a sticky blotchy skin with spikes all over,
With an eagle's claws and the cunning of man,
And you may get the right portrait of a dragon.
When piqued, it spits out poison and liquid fire.
Then matching its riveting shape and size
It has great appetite and a lecherous nature.
It can kill and eat any creature and terrorize
A country. It often kidnaps the maidens fair.

These dragons have a particular fascination
For some famous sites of ancient civilization.
They are found in China, Greece and Japan;
In India, Rome, Indonesia, Tibet and Babylon.

It was generally considered a sacred duty
Of a hero to slay or to overpower a dragon
To bring peace and save a lady from captivity.
Sometimes a god or an angel vied with man
To lock horns with and kill a famous dragon.
In Christian lore, for their biblical association,
Dragons are considered the sidekicks of Satan,
In old China the dragon symbolized the yang,
The energetic male principle of the Universe.
Now it's a part of their flag, folklore and song.
The dragon blazon suggests antiquity and force.

As Greek cosmogony reveals: in the beginning
Different species of dragons came into being.
When Gaeae saw her own children, the Giants
Being destroyed by Zeus and other Olympians,

She raised an ultimate monster called Typhoeus
Whom she'd borne a long time ago to Tartarus.
Reptilian heads sprang from his each shoulder,
From his each maw issued out a black tongue
And his orifices spurted out molten lava-like fire.
Hundreds of vipers sprouted up from his strong
Body that petered into a snaky, prehensile tail.
In size, he was perhaps as big as a blue whale.
He had the impenetrable coat of a rhinoceros,
And bristling darts of an aggressive porcupine.
Some gods, when they saw him, fled Olympus.
But Zeus alone fought bravely an internecine

Battle with him and, by the help of his thunder,
Was able to overpower and tear him asunder.

Legend has it that Cadmus killed one dragon
And sowed its teeth on a stretch of tilled earth.
Anon, out of those furrows sprang up a legion
Of veteran warriors livid with warlike wrath.
Without any apparent provocation whatsoever
They attacked and went on killing one another
As if the aim of their life was to fight and to kill.
Many heads rolled; a lot of blood they did spill.

A few tough blokes luckily survived the scuffle;
They were the first fathers of the Theban people.
As they sprouted up from a dead dragon's fang,
Their descendants became aggressive and strong.

The Dragon that watched over the Golden Fleece
Was one of the better-known monsters of its day.
Jason, helped by Medea, the princess of Colchis,
Outmaneuvered that dragon in a roundabout way.

Jason was the first hero born in the Greek soil
To cross the Hellespont, and win that rare spoil
Known as the Golden Fleece. It was a treasure
Which only the bravest adventurer could aspire

To possess, because that task entailed such odds
As could be overcome only with the help of gods.

A sad event is tagged with that Golden Wool;
That's true of all things unique and beautiful.
Boeotia was then ruled by king Athamas;
The wife of Athamas was called Nephele.
They had one young son named Phrixus
And one charming daughter named Helle.
Then the king wanted to have a new wife.
He married Ino and she brought him strife.

Stepmothers, mostly in the myths and folklores,
Behave most often like self-seeking predators.
Ino, true to her tribe, circumvented a situation
Where the king would be forced to offer his son
As a sacrifice to save his country from drought
And for the helpless king there was no way out.
But just before that bloody sacrifice was done,
Before the wily queen could execute her plan,
Hermes sent down a ram with the Golden Fleece.
That animal carried Phrixus and Helle to Colchis.
While on the way, the ram of Hermes careened
Over the Black Sea in nearly supersonic speed.
The little princess Helle felt very giddy and tense.
Most probably, she had a bout of flight sickness.
Or it could well be a case of dozing or inattention.
Nothing of course could be known now for certain.
Whatever the real cause of her mishap might be:
She slid off the sheep's back and fell into the sea.
People named the place Hellespont after her fall
To commemorate it, and to serve a warning to all.

As soon as he arrived at Colchis, prince Phrixus
Sacrificed Hermes's ram and offered it to Zeus.
Then he skinned the ram and offered the Fleece
To Aeaetes who was, then, ruling over Colchis.
The Fleece was an object of unusual splendour;
Nothing in the world did match it, a real wonder.

In a sacred grove, it glowed like a slice of sunset,
Watched over by a magical dragon that never slept.

During that period, the king of Thessaly was Aeson;
He had a nephew named Pelias, a son called Jason.
Pelias conspired, usurped the throne treacherously
And banished his uncle king Aeson from Thessaly.
Ere he was deposed, the king had entrusted his son
Jason to a teacher of many skills, the Centaur Chiron.

When Jason became a young man expert in warfare,
He set out to punish Pelias and search out his father.
On his way to Thessaly, he helped a frail old woman
With a lovely peacock, who was in a trying situation,
By helping her cross a swiftly flowing mountain river.
She was goddess Hera who was testing his character.

He lost one of his shoes while trudging in the current
(We will know presently what his loss of shoe meant.)

Jason limped into Pelias's court with one foot shod,
Wearing a leopard-skin jacket and carrying a sword.
Pelias panicked, for that outlandishly attired stranger
Reminded him of the prophesy of the Speaking Oak
Which, when consulted, had advised him to beware
Of a stranger who would be a chip off the old block

With leopard-skin jacket, a sword and a single shoe.
That man would chuck him out and be his fatal foe.

When questioned about his lineage, identity,
As well as the immediate purpose of his visit,
Jason demanded that the king Pelias hand over
The throne that belonged to Aeson, his father.

Jason must have been a very naive young man
To believe he'd get a throne if he asked for one.
He claimed his kingdom and that was in order,
But the usurper Pelias was cautious and clever.
He agreed to oblige Jason, but wanted to scuttle

The transfer of power by making it conditional.
The throne of Thessaly, he said, I will relinquish
If you can bring the Golden Fleece from Colchis.
That Fleece is a Greek treasure, it belongs to us;
It was only given away by our kinsman, Phrixus.

Well, Pelias, said Jason, if I recover that Fleece,
You must give us back our kingdom and vanish.
I know you're a sly usurper, a traitor and a fraud,
But I have no intention to shed a kinsman's blood.
If you go back on your word and cheat it on me,
Then what I can do with this sword, you will see.
Pelias had a merry laugh when Jason was gone,
And bitched: Ha, I'm sending food to a dragon.
Believe me, I am yet to see a greater simpleton.

Jason made preparations to build a gigantic ship.
His young mind was raring to go on a foreign trip.
The Speaking Oak of Dodona told him to bid Argus,
A famed ship-maker, to make a ship with fifty oars.
Argus built the ship using his skills and fine timber.
The Greeks had never made such a big ship before.
Then Jason spread the news of his voyage in Greece
Asking the bravest of the brave to join his enterprise.
Legendary heroes who'd already proved their power,
As well as avid young heroes athirst for adventure,
Bestirred themselves and joined force with Jason:
Hercules, Atalanta, Orpheus, Theseus… and so on.
Hera gave Jason blessings through the Figurehead;
Some fifty Argonauts set out - with water and bread.
Many adventures they had en route, quite daunting.
The Argonauts whose courage matched their mission

Encountered them all successfully without flinching,
Though they had some moments of crisis and tension.

Hercules dropped out of the group on the way,
Because, as reports say, he lost his errand boy
He brought with him to serve him from Greece.
He was sore and couldn't care less for the Fleece.

However, at present it can't be known for certain
Whether Hercules, an invincible, passionate man,
Opted out, or they knowingly had left him behind.
The Argonauts knew he was a hero of special kind,
And had they voyaged with that secret son of Zeus,
They might have had a marginal role as the Chorus
In Greek plays. With Hercules at a calling distance,
No adventure might have looked so very dangerous.
They didn't join the enterprise to be mere onlookers
Of one hero's adventures, and only to pull the oars.

The Argonauts, indeed, had a journey full of events,
They fought against giants, birds, men and elements.
To help unhappy Phineus, a condemned blind king,
They fought with the three Harpies, those stinking
Snatchers of food with the hag-faces, and feathers,
Talons, bills and greed of carcass-gulping vultures.

They were attacked and injured by a flock of birds
That moulted in the air the feathers sharp as goads;
Like hail, their arrow-like feathers kept on falling
On them. Advised by kind Hera at the Figurehead,
They started beating their swords on their shining
Bronze shields. Those attacking birds quickly fled
Surprised by the sudden din, confused by the clatter,
For they were not able to know what was the matter.

They met the Sirens who hid killer motives beneath
Their suave, seductive exterior and pleasant voice;
The Argonauts escaped by the skin of their teeth,
Because of Orpheus's music and resourcefulness.

They fought like devils with the six-headed giants,
Brained some, sent others scurrying to mountains.
They came to Lemnos, the land of the termagants
Who had already killed all their husbands and sons,
Without sparing their grandfathers and male infants.

Those fierce women parleyed with the Argonauts,
But quite surprisingly, they did not cut their throats.
Miss Atalanta, who was so famously mysogamous,
When asked to comment on the women of Lemnos,
Reacted: Those women of Lemnos made a blunder
By throwing their babies away with the bath water.
Like me, they could well have stayed out of marriage.
For good or bad, mates, I do not like such carnage.
None liked that, but all mulled over the repercussion
Of such male-genocide, of the all-female population.
One said: Are all women here so completely lesbian?
And another: Even then, you can't justify such action.

To furnish their ships with provisions and fresh water,
On many strange shores they had to drop the anchor.
They faced many situations, daunting and diabolical;
But by dint of their courage, they overcame them all.

Then the Argonauts reached the land of their quest.
They were worn to a frazzle. And while taking rest,
They heard gossips concerning the Golden Fleece,
How Phrixus was carried to Colchis from Greece;
About the Sleepless Dragon that belched out fire
And gobbled down all creatures that came too near.

The king initially gave a warm reception to Jason
And his crew; gave them food and accommodation;
But when he learnt that the purpose of the visitors
Was to take away the Golden Fleece, he got cross.
He considered Jason an enemy, a clever trespasser.
He quickly turned hostile and was loath to brook
Jason's insolence and grant him his grand desire.
He even tried to kill them all by hook or by crook.

The king had two bulls that couldn't be held in leash.
They had bronze horns; their nostrils spewed out fire.
"Jason!" he said slyly, "You want to take the Fleece?
First, you give us a proof of your ability and valour.
Then we will believe that you're a true adventurer
Who can try his strength against the Dragon there.

This night you'd have to yoke my bulls to a plough
And dig up a two-acre plot ere the crack of dawn;
If you succeed, we would gladly permit you to go
To the grove to combat with the Sleepless Dragon."

Some of his mates weren't amused by that news:
They said: "Jason, those bulls must be ferocious,
That Sleepless Dragon must be incredibly huge.
Insomniacs, you know, are naturally pugnacious.
You must be an overweening and irrational man
To believe you can conquer or kill a real dragon.
Dragons may be good stuff for fables and fiction,
But to close with a living dragon won't be fun.
Now it is high time we should pack up and quit
This place. Forget the Fleece, man, we mean it."

Jason was determined to get the Golden Fleece
And he was prepared to die to actualize his wish.
At that moment, Cupid, the cute boy of Aphrodite,
Came to Jason's aid. As a catalyst, he did expedite
The acts of seizing and carrying off the Golden Fur,
More by magic, less by hero's courage and power.

Aeaetes the king of Colchis had a young daughter
Named Medea who was a sorceress of high calibre.
No sooner did that princess cast her eye on Jason
Than was smitten with an uncontrollable passion,
Crazing about that strapping and brave young man
Who, as the leader, was more visible than the rest,
She arranged a tryst with him in a lonely mansion.
There she assured him that she would try her best
To help him yoke the formidable bulls to the plough
And obtain the Golden Fleece by tricking the monster,
If he promised to wed and take her to Greece in tow;
That she would help him even by fleecing her father.

The princess seemed unusually forward and eager.
Initially, he viewed her with suspicion and flinched.
But later on he mellowed, and agreed to marry her

And take her to Greece. Their deal was clinched.
She became his true ally and trusted companion.
She helped him yoke the brazen bulls of Vulcan.
Then she guided him to the grove sacred to Mars.
There the Golden Fleece hung from an oak branch,
Shining with its golden glory like a shower of stars,
A stalactite of beaten gold, like the mane of Pegasus.
Beneath that gnarled oak, the dragon kept its watch.

Jason swaggered ahead to challenge the monster
With his sword, but Medea advised him to forbear
And not to step into the dragon's enchanted sphere.
"Even the bravest fly," she said, "can't kill a spider.
Although you are an adventurous and strong man,
You must know: the better part of valour is caution.
Targets and occasions may vary, but here at least,
You cannot take on a rhino-like crustaceous beast
With your ordinary, though trusty, piece of steel
That cannot scratch its outer layer, let alone kill.
If this Dragon were such an easy-to-kill creature,
It wouldn't have been trusted with such a treasure."

Then fearing lest the hero should take umbrage
And take her words as an aspersion on his courage,
She added in a sweet tone: "You see, brave Jason,
Dragons are highly endangered rarities of creation.
A dragon, you see, doesn't produce another dragon.
Precisely for that reason, they may face extinction
If heroes and gods make them their common target
And destroy them just to prove that they are great.
I will sing a soothing song and apply a magic potion
Which can put it in a state of suspended animation.
That'll enable you to get away with the golden wool,
Now, please, do sheathe your sword and play it cool."

A song did what flagons of wine couldn't have done.
It lulled into sleep the chronically insomniac dragon.

Jason with the Fleece

She prodded Jason softly and beckoned him to take
The Fleece. But he was trying his best to keep awake,
As her hypnotic song had made him a bit comatose.
He started at her touch, looked over. His blood froze
As he saw the massive dragon stretched before him
Like a Leviathan, granite-hard, awesome and grim.
He temporized, for it ill became a man of honour
To acquire a treasure by crouching like a burglar.
But the occasion was not ideal for such a debate.
So he grabbed at the Fleece before it was too late.

Jason and his Argonauts safely repaired to Greece
With the princess Medea and the purloined Fleece.
But Pelias the king of Thessaly turned out a fraud.
He flatly refused to hand over his crown to Jason.
In fine, the dishonest king went back on his word.
Medea, once again, intervened in the disputation
And helped Jason regain his father's lost throne.

Time does not stay put as soon as a story is ended.
Things change for better or worse, and get blended
With each other. Whatever happened to Jason later

Could make many more stories, both sweet and bitter.
Medea, who had cheated her father to help her lover,
Waxed crazy when Jason denied his affection to her.

She was not the type of wife who'd forgive or chide
Her husband when her husband takes her for a ride.
She killed her sons and consorted with another man
To avenge herself on her unloving husband Jason.

As regards the story of Jason and his Argonauts,
Mythmakers had passed down conflicting reports.
So people of ancient Greece carried the impression
That Jason'd won the Fleece by killing the Dragon.
The Argonauts, hoping to bask in the reflected glory
Of their hero, might have circulated that false story.
But the Sleepless Dragon lives and thrives out there
Galling mankind like the recondite force of a desire,
Like an occulted guilt, as a portentous fear or doubt.
When the night dims the earth, it stealthily comes out
Of its lair, peeping into our slumber like a nightmare,
Scouting around the world for its purloined treasure.
That is perhaps why we are filled with an eerie fright
When rocks and bushes assume shapes, begin to stir
Like creatures, and when things go bump in the night.

****

The Hydra and Hercules

The Hydra was the daughter of Echidna and Typhon
And a sibling of the Chimaera and the Nemean Lion.
She dwelt in the marshlands of Lerna at Peloponnese;
She had nine snakeheads (one immortal) of huge size.
Her breath was poisonous; her mouth shot jets of fire;
She resembled a giant squid; insatiable was her hunger.
Every night she used to forage for food and invaded
Human habitations; people there felt very insecure,
Fearing each day to be their last day, some even fled
Their hamlets, frightened by that man-eating predator.
Those people believed that the Hydra was invincible
And, for that, there would be no end to their trouble.

It so happens in the world, as well as in the fable
That when a vicious, blood-thirsty man or monster
Appears, and becomes powerful and unmanageable,
A counter, benign presence with formidable power
Incarnates to challenge and overpower his authority
To restore goodness and to bring peace to the society.

Mother Nature, it seems, takes as much care
To engender a hero as to engender one villain;
So that the labour becomes worthy of its hire
And the slayer becomes worthy of the slain.

To kill the Hydra of Lerna it required a Hercules
Who occupied, in the Greek lore, a unique place.
Let's know something about this man of action
Who seemed to be a god and a man rolled into one.

Amphitryon, at the time, was the king of Mycenae.
The name of his newly married bride was Alcmena.
Inadvertently, he killed his wife's father Electryon
Who happened to be his uncle, hence his kinsman.
For shedding a kin's blood, he needed purification.
So he went with his bride to the Theban king Creon.

Hercules and the Hydra

Amphitryon took a vow not to deflower his spouse
Until he conquered the kingdom of the Teleboans.
It seems, against Teleboans he had an ancient grouse.
His host Creon supplied him with soldiers and arms.
Amphitryon won the battle. Then riding in a carriage
He repaired to Thebes to consummate his marriage.
But, meanwhile, a calamity of extraordinary nature,
And of a far-reaching import, befell this conqueror.

Zeus, the chief god, who had an unquenchable desire
For earthly beauties, entered Alcmena's bed chamber
Looking exactly like her war-worn hubby Amphitryon.
"O my God," said she, "you came back all of a sudden.
That's fine, but why didn't you announce your return?"

"Look, darling," he said, "I came from the battlefield
Straightaway. Here's my red sword; here's my shield.
I won the battle; then quietly I slipped out of my tent.
I have another battle to win; you can guess my intent.
I didn't announce my return and stand on ceremony.
I wanted to give you a surprise. That was the reason."

Alcmena, poor lady, believed every word he said
And granted him the pleasures of the marriage bed.
As a single night was not enough for such delights,
Zeus stretched that single night to three full nights.
When the victorious husband arrived in full steam,
He gathered that his look-alike had anticipated him
Already on his marriage bed. Furious and curious,
Amphitryon consulted the blind prophet Tieresias
And came to know that it was no other than Zeus.
He fretted, fumed, bellowed and ground his teeth,
But finally realized nothing could be done about it.

Alcmena, inseminated twice by two Amphitryons,
In due course of time, gave birth to two baby sons.
Hercules, the first-born baby boy, she bore to Zeus,
And, to her husband Amphitryon, she bore Iphicles.

Zeus was the king of heaven and Hera was his wife.
And their marital relationship was marked by strife.
The type of conjugal life that Olympian couple led,
By human standards even, it left a lot to be desired.
Undeterred by his outraged and straitlaced spouse's
Nagging, he kept visiting pretty ladies in many guises.
He visited Danae as golden shower, Leda as a swan,
He visited Alcmena, a bride, looking just like her man,
He visited one as a gust of wind, another as an infant,
He visited Europa as a flying bull; another as an ant.

In this case particularly, he became very cavalier
And flaunted his feat in a "heavenly" get-together.
"Hear, O Olympians," he said bubbling with mirth,
"In Greece the first baby boy that touches the earth
This very night will be a man extraordinarily capable
Of killing monsters, of making impossible possible.
He'd commit blunders, perform such feats of daring
That the earthlings would never be tired of hearing.
They'd love him for his power, hate him for wrongs.
They'd celebrate his adventures in stories and songs."

He paused for effect and then resumed his narration:
"You'll be amazed to know: this boy is my own son.
Though I've fathered a good many mortals, a legion,
I would be proud of, even partial towards, this one."

His words, though they were casually spoken,
Sounded like an ego trip, a public confession.
So he hastened to make his position a bit clear
And went on: "O Olympians, I am quite aware,
Some of you are prudish and allergic to fun;
They have prejudices and a lot of inhibition;
They think I have a yen for human beauties
And indulge myself too often with frivolities.
Don't trust them. But once for all, I tell you
I am earnest, utterly faithful, and utterly true.
Don't you Olympians know that in all my life
I am monogamous and I have only one wife?
I have a strict sense of propriety and honour;
I always consider insincerity in love a crime,
That's why I've never fallen in love with more
Than one woman, I mean to say, at one time."

That was vintage Jovian stuff, tastefully spiced.
So the gods and goddesses smiled and rejoiced.
But his spouse Hera's humiliation was complete.
And she quickly decided to do something about it.
Most of these Olympians, she mused, are goatish
Suffering from either nymphomania, or satyriasis.
They stay always in a state of amoral excitement;
So any public display of my love-related torment
Would amuse them and increase their merriment.
Vulcan exposed his wife Venus's affair with Mars,
But he became a laughing-stock, his grief, a farce.

Making use of her divine agencies and powers,
Hera delayed Hercules's birth by a few hours
 By obstructing mother Alcmena's uterine exit.
Eurystheus was the first baby born that night
To some Mycenaean king known as Sthenelus.
Zeus, when he came to discover it, was furious

And found no words to express his annoyance,
For a part of his prophecy didn't come to pass.

Hercules proved his mettle even in his infancy.
The wronged wife of Zeus, who knew no mercy,
Sent two venomous serpents to swallow or bite
Alcmena's two sons. Iphicles screamed in fright
Seeing them, but Hercules held them in his grip
And squeezed them to death. It was just the tip
Of the iceberg, for he'd have many an encounter
With a number of stronger adversaries in future

Theban people thought: "This baby has the stuff
That fabled, larger-than-life heroes are made of."
But the putative father Amphitryon was anxious,
So he consulted again the old prophet Tieresias.
The prophet was able to see clearly what was up
And smilingly advised the troubled father to stop
Worrying about the well-being of his son Hercules.
"Relax, Amphitryon," he said: "Your firstborn child
Will survive all ordeals. His protector is Lord Zeus.
His prowess is incredible just as his nature is wild.
You are wrong to consider him an ordinary child
As your other son Iphicles. He is a river in flood,
With a lot of life-friendly water, and a lot of mud.
It is only the beginning; he'll face many troubles,
Kill many ogres and cleanse the dirtiest of stables.
When grown up, this child will choose hard labour
In lieu of a life of creature comforts and pleasure."

In due course, he grew up, received good training
In the art of war, especially in archery and wrestling.
It was then thought necessary for a man of action
To cultivate some fine arts like music and elocution.
Young Hercules made an unmusical use of his lyre.
With it he struck and killed, Linus, his music teacher.
For that absolutely uncalled-for and homicidal action,
He had to sojourn as an exile on the Mt. Cithaeron.

A Statue of Hercules

There he began his eventful career by slaying a lion
That was preying regularly on the cattle of Thespius,
The king of Thespiae. So, the king indulged Hercules,
His benefactor, by proffering him not only hospitality
But also his fifty daughters, each daughter for a night.

"Now, Zeus, I believe your bastard seems to be pure",
Commented Hera with a malicious, carping humour,
"As I see, in such amatory feats at least, that bugger
Is surely going to equal the track records of his father."
Zeus, however, heard her, but he did not take offence;
He knew: as a husband, he should cultivate patience
And tolerance, and put up with his wife's mood-flares
In order to contain her, while carrying on his affairs.

While residing in Thebes, Hercules led an invasion
Against the Minyans. He wanted to free King Creon

From paying tributes to that state; it was a necessity
Imposed on Thebes in observance of some old treaty.
As expected, the Minyans suffered a crushing defeat,
And so, they didn't claim tributes as a matter of right.
Grateful Creon, much impressed by Hercules' courage,
Gave his comely daughter Megara to him in marriage.
Megara proved an ideal wife. They had three children,
But Hera, implacable as ever, again played the villain.
She afflicted Hercules with a bout of sudden insanity,
And he murdered his wife and three children in that fit.
He soon recovered and when he saw what he'd done,
He plunged in grief, suffered from severe depression.

In the Greek world, it was considered a grave sin
If a man murdered his own guest, or his blood-kin.
Distraught and lost, he wished to know his future
From the Sybil of Apollo. She advised him to repair
Immediately to King Eurystheus for his purification,
Because he'd incurred unforgivable sins by his action.
The Sybil of Apollo at Delphi told him: "O Hercules,
You're in the bad books of Hera, the consort of Zeus.
She had sent those serpents; she turned you insane,
And made you murder your good wife and children.
The king Eurystheus, who was born just a few hours
Earlier, will impose upon you twelve difficult labours.

Using your skill and strength, try to perform them all.
No man, as long as he lives, can become an immortal."

Hercules visited king Eurystheus for his purification.
First, the king ordered him to kill the Nemean Lion.
Hercules had no choice, but to do the king's bidding.
His first labour turned out very tough and daunting.
Lions are considered the strongest of all predators;
In addition, that Lion had the derma of a rhinoceros,
Which was impregnable. So his arrows and spears
Couldn't scratch its surface, let alone pierce its side.
Hercules had to throttle it. Then he removed its hide,
Dried it, tanned it, stitched it and used it as his tunic.
As he strode into the king's court wearing that attire,

Male courtiers trembled and all women fled in panic.
Then he was told to kill the Hydra as his next labour.

The Hydra was a monster with a chilling reputation;
He found it more redoubtable than the Nemean lion,
For, with nine hoods, she was nine monsters in one.
Again, to add to his disadvantage as well as labour,
Hera sent off promptly a gigantic crab to the marsh
To join forces with the Hydra, her favourite monster.

The Hydra

The site where the Hydra lived was a treacherous
Bog which could suck in and drown any creature
Who dared step into it. So, Hercules had to force
The amphibian to come out of it, to the solid land.
He pestered her with ordinary missiles and arrows.
The peeved Hydra, however, could not understand
Why a poor fellow was inviting his own destruction
By teasing her. She clambered out, spewing poison,
And, stretching her tentacles, attacked the attacker.
Hercules brandished his mighty club and struck her
He soon realized that it was sheer wastage of labour,

Because his club bounced off the Hydra's scaly body.
Then he unsheathed his sword, and cut off one head,
But to his amazement, he saw two hoods were ready
To attack him, sprouting up from one wounded bed.

"You can't kill her like that, uncle", said a voice.
He veered round, and saw his own nephew Iolaus.
"Iolaus, you'll tell me later what brought you here;
First tell me what is so special about this monster.
I am afraid if I hack down her nine darned heads
She may turn into a creature with eighteen heads."

"You're true", assured the youth with a knowing smile.
Hercules gasped: "O Iolaus, how to tackle this miracle?"
"Don't worry; I know the trick. We'll make it together."
Assured Iolaus: "I shall set the dry tree yonder on fire.
We'll be able to prevent such dangerous proliferation
Of tentacles by burning quickly the wounded portion.
So, keep her somehow busy; she must stay on land
Until I come back and join you with a burning brand."
Hercules thanked him a lot, and resumed his fight
With the multi-headed Hydra. It was a fearful sight
To see her snaky tentacles, spread out far and near,
Lolling out forked tongues, spouting poison and fire.
The animal that Hera set on him, that terrible Crab,
Pounced on Hercules, but he brained it with his club.
When Hera saw her favourite Crab so easily undone,
She placed it in the sky as the Cancer Constellation.

Soon after, the resourceful Iolaus joined his hand
With Hercules, holding aloft a long burning brand.
No sooner a severed tentacle dropped on the ground,
Than Iolaus applied the burning brand to the wound.
At last, Hercules hacked the last hood with a stroke
And buried it promptly under a huge chunk of rock.
At that moment, Hercules committed an act of folly
For which he paid in the last part of his life, dearly.
Little realizing that he was multiplying his sorrows,
In the Hydra's noxious blood, he dipped his arrows.

Poisoning of arrows was one of the cowardly tricks,
Which were universally disapproved by the Greeks.

Years later, he shot one of those arrows at a Centaur
While the latter was carrying Deineira across a river.
The Centaur avenged himself by gifting her an apron
Soaked in his blood infected with the Hydra's poison,
Telling her to use it on her husband as a potent charm
When she would feel his love for her was not so warm.
"Your man," said the dying Centaur, "has a tendency
To be turned on by as many women as he would see.
Whenever you'll suspect that he is wenching around
And has lost his affection for you, send him this tunic.
Then, he will be as faithful to you as your pet hound
And will pine for your love, for this cloth is magic.
Once he puts it on, were he in the amorous embrace
Of the comeliest and the stickiest woman of Greece,
His love for you will singe him like Vulcan's furnace
And he would spurn her and long for conjugal bliss."

Deineira did not want to lose Hercules's affection
And preserved the tunic as her prized possession.
Years after, she heard some true or false rumours
About her husband Hercules's extramarital affairs.
Moved by grief and wishing to regain his affection,
To Hercules she sent off that magic cloth of poison,
Requesting him to wear it, and waited for his return.
As soon as Hercules put on that venomous garment,
His whole body was on fire; he was in fiery torment;
It scorched into his skin like nitric acid and did rend
Him apiece. He met an abrupt and excruciating end.

Hera took kindly to Hercules when he gave up his life
On earth and entered Olympus. She offered him nectar.
She offered her own daughter Hebe to him as his wife
And threw a gala party in Olympus in Hercules' honour.

****

The Gorgon Medusa and Perseus

When we are happy and chance on a smiling face,
The world blooms for us, becomes a magical place
Where even our fantasies begin to make some sense.
The storm clouds that range menacingly in the east
Flash out rainbows, a frugal meal tastes like a feast.
Happy Jack drives sullen Jill in tandem to the park;
Fresh breeze and whispering lovers revive her spirit.
She throws off her hands and yodels: "Hey, my Jack,
Life looks so delicious, so crisp. Come, let's have it."

But when we are sad and meet a scowling harridan,
We are gripped by an inexplicable fear; depression
Descends on us like a funerary pall; the flame of joy
Flickers and then goes out; our smile turns to a grin;
We have a feeling that life's fobbing us off with a toy.
We wanted unalloyed gold; but found pinchbeck tin;
The moon is not always round; the meat is all gristle.
We have all the causes to be sad, mad and to grizzle.
The breeze blows with the stench of rotting flowers,
The smoke rising from smoldering pyres chokes us.
It's so, because that unhappy face is a stern reminder
That our world is full of grave uncertainties and pain;
That man, though he ups the ante hopefully, is a loser
In the casino of life, a captive in this sky-roofed den.

The world is full of people who love to torment others.
Their purpose is to lessen happiness by making a fuss
About coming disasters, by giving us doomsday blues
By supplying us unasked the bottled imps of sad news

These grouches actually get some a sadistic pleasure
By making other people unhappy, by hawking despair.
Perpetually preoccupied with the seamy side of things,
They keep telling: Pleasures you chase are red herrings.
 Such a hag was Medusa, one of the Gorgon sisters.
Her wrinkled wry face – she'd many wrinkles indeed –
Wore the smudge of old sorrows, unfulfilled desires,

Unrelieved bitterness arising out of hatred and greed.
In place of hairs, she had living serpents that spread
Their hoods in different directions, hissing, popping
In and out their forked tongues, to protect the head
That sprouted them. Her gaze was literally petrifying.
It was improbable that, with such an awful coiffeur,
She could encourage a man or god to be her lover.
But in spite of her old age and scary physiognomy
She was not lacking in caring and good company.

Medusa the Gorgon

Her immortal sisters, named Stheno and Euryale,
Shared a dark cave with Medusa and constantly
Watched over her, so that no one could harm her
They feared her death would make them lonelier.
Her two immortal Gorgon siblings were ageless,
But Medusa was an ancient and mortal woman.
Their faces were so hideous and full of distress
That their sight could turn onlookers into stone.

That's why the Gorgons were feared and hated.
Their congealed despair could suck the life-sap
Out of all living beings, just as the deserts sated
Their thirst by soaking up streams. Such mishap
Had not befallen to many, as the legends tell us,
For those Gorgons had stowed away themselves
In a gloomy cavern at the end of the earth, across
The broad stream of Oceanus near the Hesperides.

Self-quarantined, like the patients of certain diseases,
They lived in a cave at Kisthene, a land of rockroses.
As they never wandered off from their secret hideouts;
Even the gods couldn't know about their whereabouts.
Only living beings that knew where the Gorgons stay
Were their three sibling sisters, known as the Graeae.

So much about the Gorgons; now about Perseus:
He was one of the noblest of the mythical heroes.

Once upon a time the prosperous kingdom of Argos
Was ruled over by a credulous man named Acrisius.
In those days people most often consulted Oracles
For everything, and invited upon them real troubles.
Acrisius, like others, was curious to know his future.
Apollo's Oracle told him: "Acrisius, know for sure,
Your own grandson will murder you sooner or later."

Determined to botch the machinations of his fate,
He put his only daughter Danae in a brass garret.
His arguments for taking such a step were straight:
If his only daughter would not cohabit with a man,
She won't conceive, and he won't have a grandson.
If he had no grandson, he'd have no reason to fear
Any other man. So he would go on living for ever.

In such situations, paradoxes were rather obvious:
They trusted Oracles, but tried to prove them false.

Zeus, as already described, has a libidinal yen
For terrestrial beauties, mostly virginal women.

In other words, the human world was his oyster.
To match his immortal appetite, he had the power
To assume any shape he liked and to go anywhere.
He mated with Danae looking like a golden shower.
The gestation time over, Danae gave birth to a son,
So Acrisius became a grandpa and a worried man.
Now, he had to protect himself from his grandson.
The king was also worried about his own honour,
For his unmarried daughter had become a mother.
About one thing, however, he couldn't be certain:
How could his daughter conceive without a man?
Determined to save his life as well as his honour,
He thrust his daughter and his grandson Perseus
Into a wooden chest, and floated it down a river.
The wooden chest drifted downwards to Seraphos
Where Polydectes, an amorous man, was the ruler.

A woman with youth and beauty is like a musk deer
Who is oft ruined because of her precious treasure.
Danae was pretty, so Polydectes wanted to lay her
But she refused categorically to have him as a lover.
So, both the mother and son had to scrape a living
By hard work, and were often harassed by the king.
Now, let's know about the immediate provocation
Which forced Perseus to go gunning for the Gorgon.

We'll form a clear impression of this natural hero
If we knew what forced him to take up this labour.
The son of a victimized, exiled and single mother,
Persues didn't even know who was his real father.
His mother herself was ignorant of the whole affair,
As Zeus ravished her looking like a golden shower.

The single mother was beautiful and defenseless.
So, many unpleasant situations she had to face.
Most men have a crush on the woman with a past.
She'd to keep them off, though not without a cost.
She was forced to antagonize the king Polydectes
By not succumbing to his many amorous advances.

So, the spurned king, whenever he got an occasion,
Harassed and humiliated the poor lady and her son.

Once, Polydectes invited Perseus to his wedding,
And demanded he must gift him a precious thing,
Knowing well that his guest was not in a position
To arrange a precious gift to fulfill his condition.

He pleaded: "Your Highness knows that I am poor.
I have nothing save my youth, courage and honour."

"You only exaggerate; it's a fine piece of boasting.
It seems your youth and courage avail you nothing,
As they are not worth even a gift," taunted the king,
"Now, save your honour; present us a fabulous thing."

"Polydectes", Perseus retorted, "you are a bad host.
You have insulted a guest. But I will try my utmost
To be worthy of your condition, of what you just said.
I won't show up until I bring you the Gorgon's head."
With that promise, he left the court without waiting
To hear some more unkind taunts from the mean king.
He set off without even bidding farewell to his mother;
Decided to go home only after avenging his dishonour.

To fetch the Gorgon Medusa's head! It was a whale
Of a vow. But he turned out a whale of a hero, as well.

A common man, if humiliated, weeps, fumes or frets.
He sometimes injures himself or the people he hates.
But a hero performs something incredible and singular,
Which benefits humanity while restoring his honour.

That very moment, Perseus set out on the adventure:
To kill Medusa, without knowing a thing about her.
When he dozed off, Athena visited him in a dream.
"Perseus, you are daydreaming," she upbraided him:
"Tell me, what on earth do you think you are doing?
Even I do not know where the Gorgons are staying.

You think you will find them out by mere guesswork?
You may search and search, yet be wide of the mark."

"You know," said Perseus (in his dream, of course),
"Actually I am a peace-loving man, not pugnacious.
True, I've no idea about the place of these Gorgons;
I know they have power to change people into stones.
Whether my task is self-imposed, or by someone else,
Now it is too late to back out; it would be a disgrace.
I must bring Medusa's head; it's my word of honour.
I am not bothered if I turn to stone in the encounter."

The goddess appreciated him for what he said.
Walking up to him, she softly touched his head.
"Perseus," Athena said sweetly, "I have come here
To assist you. I help those whose hearts are pure;
Those who are daring; and those who seek honour
By performing incredible feats, by courting danger.
Frankly, young dreamer, I am very much pleased
To find you so charmingly different, so determined.
If you want to know, you're in fact my halfbrother.
Your mother Danae will bear me out, if you ask her
 About the brass garret and her esoteric encounter
With someone who visited her as a golden shower.
But I've another motive. It may sound a bit selfish.
I want Gorgon Medusa's head for my bronze aegis.
You will have to behead her without looking at her.
So I give you my shield, which will act as a mirror.
You must try to behead her with a backhand stroke.
More assistance will flow in. I wish you good-luck."

Perseus woke up from his pleasant dream,
And found a shining shield lying near him.
He tried it on his chest kept it in a safe place
And sat cupping his chin, adoring the goddess.
Happy thoughts engaged him; soon it was night.
In his second dream, Hermes paid him a visit.

"I know what you're up to, man," said the god,
"I have come here to give you my magic sword.

It has the power to slice up any object it strikes,
Be it a boulder, a Gorgon's neck or metal spikes.
I do not know where these Gorgon sisters stay.
Extract that secret from their sisters, the Graeae.
They are loyal to Gorgon siblings, very obstinate.
So you'll have to force them to reveal their secret.
You may ask me: Force them to do it? But how?
Don't worry, I will tell you a thing or two I know.
These Grey Goddesses are born with grey hair,
They look alike and dress in bright saffron attire.
One more hint I shall give you about the Graeae;
You should use it resourcefully and carry the day.
The Graeae have been cursed from birth to share
Only a single eye and one tooth, one after the other.
A denture with one tooth is not useful for chewing,
Yet they love it dearly for one is better than nothing.
Three sisters sharing a single eye, is a great bother;
Yet they bank on it to see the world and each other.

Perseus woke up, looked around and saw the sword.
Then he remembered the friendly words of the god.
He applied himself to his search with double vigour
When he knew the gods were interested in his affair.

He reached the cavern where lived the Graeae
Who used to see the world with a mutual eye.
He waited outside untill they were fast asleep,
For that would make it easier for him to creep
Into their cavern and steal their eye and tooth
And force them to reveal their guarded truth.
Perseus knew such an arm-twisting procedure
Was very mean and quite unbecoming of a hero,
But he had not any other way to know the secret
Which would enable him to arrive at his target.
They stored their eye and tooth in a wall alcove
Before they fell asleep and soon began to snore.

Perseus stole their limbs and put them in a glove
And stood there patiently until the night was over.

Afraid of forfeiting their abilities to see and to chew,
They told him all he wanted to know, and they knew
Of their sister Medusa. Besides, they'd little to fear
On her account as she'd more than adequate power
 To protect her own self from a human adventurer.
Besides, there were two other sisters to protect her.

Armed with Pallas Athena's impregnable aegis
And Herme's long sword that never goes amiss
And now furnished with the Graeae's information,
Perseus felt confident to accomplish his mission.
It is said that a job well started is nearly half done,
And when fortune favours (it favours a brave man),
An impromptu move turns out to be the proper one.
Perseus misinterpreted Graeae's route descriptions
And blundered into the land of the Hyperboreans.

It was believed men of another land couldn't know
The blessed land of the Hyperboreans, let alone go.
All the denizens there were charming and full of fun,
With hearts that always brimmed over with affection.
People there caroused, dined, danced and lived a life
Full of peace and communal love; they knew no strife.
As the Hyperboreans were winsome, happy and wise,
Their land could have matched our idea of a Paradise.
They welcomed Perseus with smiles of cordiality
And he was overwhelmed by their warm hospitality.

When the hosts learnt from him about his mission,
They supplied him with some useful information.
They gave him a cap that would make him invisible
If he wore it and a special sack stretchy and flexible
To keep the severed head of Medusa as a precaution,
For if displayed, the head could turn people to stone.
To enable him to escape from the immortal Gorgons,
They gave him a pair of sandals winged like swans.
If the wearer told them the place he'd like to travel,
They would transport him there without any trouble.

Here we may become skeptical, and think like this:
"Blessed with Pallas Athena's impenetrable aegis,
Hermes' magic sword with its great cutting power,
A magic cap that can make one invisible as ether,
The sandals that can take the wearer everywhere
And, finally, to have the gods at a calling distance,
An ordinary man can be as adventurous as Perseus.
If he wants he can throw a challenge to Hercules,
Slay the Minotaur and behead a dozen of Gorgons."

One may make a similar disparaging observation
About Greek hero Achilles and Indian hero Arjuna:
That with such an arsenal of supernal ammunition,
An assurance of physical immunity against danger,
With Pallas Athena as a constant, caring companion
And Lord Krishna as a bosom friend and charioteer,
Any man can become a hero without taking any risk.
He can overcome all obstacles with ease and whisk
Away great dangers. When the celestial proximity
Ensured a human being foolproof invulnerability,
He'd feel safe, that feeling would carry him along,
And he may win many wars while crooning a song.
When you happen to be in the good books of gods,
You never miss the mark; you win against all odds.
They stretch the small circle into a circumference,
Which holds you and what you treat as your target;
Rough and tricky terrains turn level like highways,
And they even rein in time's chariot if you are late.
Such an argument is pleasing, yes, but not so right.
Maybe, it is like putting the cart before the horse.
Gods help only after the hero has proved his might.
Perseus, when he set off on his ambitious course,

Had carried a brave heart, but an ordinary sword
And had not been assured of any help by any god.

Adequately provided for and against all dangers
Perseus took leave of the friendly Hyperboreans.
Balancing on his swan-like sandals, away he sped
To the remote spot where the Gorgon sisters stayed.

The land was called Kisthene or the Roses of Stone.
There, three Gorgons- Medusa, Euryale and Stheno -
Lived in a large cavern turned into a loft conversion.

Standing at the cave's door, he heard Medusa tell
Her sisters in a dismal tone: "O Stheno! O Euryale!
Being ageless and deathless, you two never can
Understand the problems of an old mortal woman.
I had youth, grace and beauty; now they are gone;
Even though you are with me, I feel terribly alone.
I never wanted to lose my youth and my beauty;
But they have deserted me. What can I do about it?
I do not love this type of life, nor does life love me.
My life is a vulture sitting in yonder leafless tree.
My heart rankles with a grim sense of deprivation,
These wrinkles hurt like the stings of a scorpion.
I want love, but I am feared. Oh, this awful weight
Of my agony! I now believe death is the only gate
Of escape. My life here is a sheer waste of breath.
But, curiously, I am terribly afraid of facing death."

She paused, and resumed: "O Stheno, I've a feeling
Some one is out there to kill me while I'm sleeping.
I don't grudge him his honour. Death will be the end
Of my suffering. One who kills me is my true friend.
This old age is itself a disease, if you want to know,
It weakens the body, but desires multiply and grow.
I feel feverish! My head and knee-joints are aching!
Don't you hear me? Why don't you say something?
O now I know why you zealously protect your sister.
By being wretched myself, I help you feel happier."

Perseus was listening. One sister was rather sharp.
She rapped her back and told her curtly to shut up.
And another sister barked: "You are making a fuss
Over your hurts, aches and wrinkles and lost beauty.
Who wants to hear such complaints? Can't you relax?
Why on earth do you make a god of your mortality?
Didn't you know from the beginning you are mortal?
What's the big deal? Why don't you stop your prattle?

You must forgive me, Medusa, if I sound a bit rough.
Frankly, we're through with you and your crazy stuff.
You're trying to rig our sympathy with that prediction.
That we know. If you calm down, you will feel better.
Say something nice, and we'll give you our attention.
Don't you think there is a limit to our patience, dear?"

Perseus thought the speaker of these words rude.
Those angry words irreparably spoilt their mood
And brought their conversation to a sudden halt.
It was nearly midnight, and they soon fell asleep,
But those serpents on their heads were quite alert.
Perseus gathered himself, held the sword in his grip,
Donned his magic cap that rendered him transparent
And tiptoed into the cave with a sideways movement.

The cave had a slit passage; the inside of it was damp
But, luckily for Perseus, it was lighted by an oil lamp.
Were there no light, there could not be any reflection
Of Medusa's face. So, that might have foiled his plan.
Easy to imagine what would have been his condition,
If he ignorantly tried to behead an immortal Gorgon!

Some nocturnal birds sent out a frenzied scream,
Hyenas and jackals raised a loud din at a distance.
The snakes in Medusa's head snooped about him
And hissed frantically sensing a human presence.
The shield reflected Medusa's face. What a sight!
It sent a chill down his spine; he felt a bit listless
And frantic. It was the witching hour of the night.
As he saw her face reflected on the shield's surface,
He could guess that she, in her youth, was a beauty;
That a more than mortal woe has given to her face
Its deadly power; but he must kill her only for duty.

Either Athena guided his hand, or he had perfected
The skill of brandishing the sword behind his back,
He slit Medusa's throat at one go, deftly collected
The cut head and put it carefully in the elastic sack.

Before the immortal Gorgons woke up, he made off.
His magic shoes obeyed him; his flight was nonstop
He flew quite fast, but his thoughts raced still faster.
Flying intoxicated him, and he experienced a thrill
The likes of which no human being had felt before.

On his way, he wanted to rest and landed on a hill
By the sea. Little did he know that a new adventure
Was just waiting to happen to him on the seashore,
An adventure that'd bring him plenty of good luck.
He looked around and saw a damsel tied to a rock
That jutted out of the hill, and he got a real shock.
The captive lady was young, distraught and lovely,
Whose loveliness had shaded into pale melancholy.
But to Perseus she looked lovelier than Aphrodite,
Because she was in such a place, in such a plight.
Her bondage was a sure proof of her helplessness,
Her helpless condition attested to her innocence.
When nubile beauty and innocence go it together,
They have an instant impact on a young bachelor.
When Perseus and the damsel gazed at each other,
Love sprouted; their hearts started beating faster.

A woman's beauty, to a great extent, depends on
Who wears it; and it thrives on visual comparison.
Perseus found her very lovely, as of late he did see
The hideous Gorgons and the white-haired Graeae.

She was Andromeda, the daughter of king Cepheus.
Her mother Cassiopeia was pretty, but utterly vain.
She openly claimed to be lovelier than the daughters
of Nereus, known as the Nereids. She did not gain
Anything by making such a disparaging declaration,
But caused a lot of trouble to her unfortunate people.
The angry Nereids set a monster, a huge amphibian,
On her kingdom to wreak havoc with its population.
That monster killed more people than an epidemic.
It destroyed crops, killed livestock and spread panic.
An oracle prophesied that the monster would relent
If they gave it Andromeda, though she was innocent,

And had never offended the Nereids and the monster.
Now she was fastened to the rock to die like a martyr.

Perseus heard all these details from the sad princess.
She advised him to leave the place before it was night,
Before the sea monster came. The damsel in distress
Fascinated our happy achiever Perseus at first sight.
He liberated her from the bondage, and waited there
To give a taste of his heroic prowess to the predator.

They sat together and talked. Soon it was twilight.
The waves whimpered, and the beast hove in sight.
It was Jurassic in size, a frosty, aggressive predator,
Looking like a crocodile grown to a horse's height.
Perseus flinched, and Andromeda shrieked in terror.
The awesome beast glared around, rushed at them.
Perseus slew it with Hermes's sword. He was game.
Andromeda was astonished. She was unable to know
How a young man could behead a monster at one go.

Presently, Perseus escorted Andromeda to her father
Who was pleased and surprised to find his daughter.
Courtiers mobbed them inquiring anxiously about
The beast. Andromeda told them the whole story,
The feats of the Greek hero, and they heard her out.
They were grateful, and they celebrated the victory.
Perseus requested the king to give him his daughter
In marriage after telling him all about his adventure.
It was a case of prior love shading into negotiation.
The king consented. The priests blessed their union.
After a day or two, when the time was auspicious
Perseus, with his Andromeda, set off for Seraphos

Perseus and Andromeda

.Another legend gives this event a different version:
 That when Perseus beheaded Medusa the Gorgon,
A horse sprang up from her blood; it was Pegasus.
It was a flying horse that generally chose its riders.
It helped Perseus escape Medusa's immortal sisters
And then soared into the air, into the stables of Zeus.
Only once, it volunteered to be a mount of the hero
Bellerophon whose tale deserves a separate chapter.

Either wearing the sandals, or riding on Pegasus,
Perseus and Andromeda safely reached Seraphos.
Situation there had already changed for the worse:
Mother Danae was on the run, hiding somewhere.
Polydectes, with an unholy intent, was chasing her.
He learnt that the king was behaving like a ruffian;
Was flouting all norms; and had legalized extortion.
He came to know that king Polydectes at that time
Was feasting in a hall with his accomplices in crime.

On hearing that news, he rushed to the banquet hall
And, standing at the entrance, he said in a loud tone:
"O Polydectes, I promised you a gift. Do you recall?

I had promised to offer you the head of the Gorgon."
Then he hoisted aloft his literally petrifying gift
All present there veered round to have a look at it
Out of curiosity and were transformed into stone.
The people rejoiced, because the tyrant was gone.

With mother and wife, he visited his country Argos,
Wishing to be reconciled with his grandpa Acrisius
Who had done a sinister turn to him and his mother,
For trying to get rid of them by drowning in a river.
The king was alive, and still wary of his grandson.
When he came to know of Perseus's glorious return,
To a neighbouring state called Palasgiotis he did hie.
Even if extremely old, he was not at all willing to die
In the hand of Perseus, his grandson. Poor old fool!
The fellow might have saved himself a lot of trouble
If he realized that the decree of fate was irrevocable.

After a few days, the ruler of that nearby kingdom
Invited Perseus, the famed Gorgon-slayer, to come
To a funeral sport. Perseus obliged him and went
There, and participated in the discus-throw event.
When his turn came, he whirled and hurled a discus,
Which slipped from his grasp and went off its course
And hit an old onlooker on the head with great force.
It brained him instantly. Lo, the victim was Acrisius.

Perseus became the king of Argos, led an ideal life
With his single mum Danae and Andromeda his wife.
He could understand that peace was better than strife,
So he didn't get attached to his miracle possessions,
And returned the cap and shoes to the Hyperboreans.
To Athena he proffered the Gorgon Medusa's head;
To Hermes he returned with thanks the magic sword.
The people of Seraphos and Argos, when he was dead,
Constructed his statues and worshipped him as a god.

****

The Minotaur and Theseus

It is as difficult to trace back the origin of a myth
As to find one's way out of the Cretan Labyrinth.
Some say, the mythologies of human civilization
Showcase diverse stages of our mental evolution.
Myths figuratively reveal to us how, step by step,
Human desire, through the power of imagination,
Tried to circumvent impasses just to fulfill itself;
How uncanny natural phenomena troubling man
Were subjected to many a popular interpretation.
Be it what it may, those resourceful mythmakers
Of ancient Greece found a fine and apt metaphor
For their existential fears and chilling nightmares
In a man in the Labyrinth waiting for the Minotaur.

Now it is time to know how this monstrous thing,
The Minotaur, "Bull of Minos," came into being.

Cronos, like his father Uranus, was a cranky father;
He despised the children his wife Rhea did engender.
For some reasons, he treated each of them as a rival.
So he would not even touch them with a barge pole.
He swallowed five of his daughters and sons whole,
Disregarding his wife's cries and outraged sentiment.
So, Rhea hid her last-born son in the island of Crete
Just to save him from his father's pathological palate.
When that son Zeus grew up, he vanquished Cronos
And became the undisputed Ruler of the Olympians.

Once Zeus (Romans called him Jupiter) fell in love
With the princess of Sidon: Europa was her name.
He appeared to her as a bull, and carried her above
The seas to his childhood foster land Crete. His aim
Was both erotic and patriotic, for he wanted to beget
A worthy son by her, who would be the king of Crete.

A son called Minos was born from their sexual union.
He grew up to become the ruler of that island nation.

He lived happily with wife Pasiphae and Androgeos,
His son, but his fortune sadly changed for the worse.
One tricky morning, Poseidon, the god of the ocean
Offered Minos and his wife a handsome, black bull
Asking them to sacrifice it to him, that is, Poseidon.
That was a gratuitous order no doubt, but the rule
Didn't permit a mortal king to reason with divinity.

As the bull of Poseidon was extremely beautiful,
Minos and Pasiphae were unwilling to sacrifice it.
The king and the queen wondered: What a joke!
After gifting us such a fine bull, he wants it back!
Poseidon crossed his fingers and patiently waited,
But the sacrifice of the bull was endlessly delayed.
He felt cheated, waxed wroth and warned the king,
But Minos and his queen, alas, were past all caring.
They ignored the warnings of the god, not realizing
That those Olympian gods had tremendous powers
To harm men, to inflict on them unusual suffering,
And even to fire their minds with atrocious desires.

Thanks to Poseidon's grotesque machinations,
Pasiphae, the queen of Crete and wife of Minos
Fell insanely in love with, and had a huge crush
On Poseidon's sacrificial and handsome tauros.
And the offshoot of their unwieldy sexual affair
Was a crossbred beast known as the Minotaur.

To that monster with man's body and bull's head,
All living beings were fodder, all rags were red.
A protégé of the king and a scourge of Poseidon,
The Minotaur was a law unto itself, afraid of none,
And went berserk killing Cretan people just for fun.
Minos sought the succour of Daedalus, the architect
Who obliged him by building a complex structure,
Called the Labyrinth with many corridors, a perfect

Maze that could bewilder and confine any creature
Who ventured or strayed into it even once, forever.

Theseus fighting with the Minotaur

Thanks to Poseidon's grotesque machinations,
Pasiphae, the queen of Crete and wife of Minos
Fell insanely in love with, and had a huge crush
On Poseidon's sacrificial and handsome tauros.
And the offshoot of their unwieldy sexual affair
Was a crossbred beast known as the Minotaur.

To that monster with man's body and bull's head,
All living beings were fodder, all rags were red.
A protégé of the king and a scourge of Poseidon,
The Minotaur was a law unto itself, afraid of none,
And went berserk killing Cretan people just for fun.

Minos sought the succour of Daedalus, the architect
Who obliged him by building a complex structure,

Called the Labyrinth with many corridors, a perfect
Maze that could bewilder and confine any creature
Who ventured or strayed into it even once, forever.
The Labyrinth was an architectural feat, a wonder.
No sooner the bull-headed predator rushed into it
Than it was trapped, always searching for an exit.

Daedalus, we should conclude, was quite smart,
For having elevated confusion to the level of art.
Just as an idle thought, one may add a metaphor:
God treats men as Daedalus treated the Minotaur,
By confining them in a similar mind-blowing maze,
In this castle of revolving mirrors called worldly life,
Replete with misprision, a land inundated by mirage
And riddled with crisscross of reflections and strife;
A place where apparent entrances and exits abound,
Identical walled-in corridors, like wishes, are galore,
Which do not lead poor captives to any open ground,
But to an ever-enticing and ever-receding elsewhere.

On an occasion, Androgeos the only son of Minos
Paid a friendly visit to the court of the king Aegeus.
The king of Athens disregarded the diplomatic rule,
And sent his guest Androgeos in to tame a wild bull.
Androgeos was brave, but not a trained bullfighter.
He tried his best, but, alas, died in that encounter.
The outraged Minos invaded and defeated Athens,
But didn't loot the city on condition that every year
A contingent of seven young men and seven damsels
Be dispatched to Crete to be given to the Minotaur.

Now it's high time we said something about Theseus
Who ranked high among the famous Grecian heroes.
In Greece there was a tiny kingdom called Troezene,
Ringed with the natural ramparts of many a mountain.
Once that sylvan country was ruled by king Pittheus.
His daughter Aethra wedded Athenian prince Aegeus.
Aegeus, a few months after marriage, left for Athens
Where he soon became the king. But before he'd left,
He kept a gold-hilted sword and his sandals in a cleft

And covered the cleft with a ponderous slab of stone.
He left his pregnant wife Aethra with the instruction
That his son (who, of course, had not yet been born)
If and when could remove that ponderous rock alone,
He would be allowed to inherit that hidden heirloom

Aethra, when her son's youth was in full bloom,
Showed him that spot, with: "Son, see this stone;
If you are able to remove it alone, I'm sure you can,
You will find beneath it a fine sword and footgear.
They are for you. Your father has kept them there."
Theseus warmed himself up, took a deep breath,
And with the maiden attempt lifted that monolith.

He held the sword, shod his feet with the sandals
And set off shortly after to meet up with his father.
He took the route that crawled with the vandals
And bandits who had unleashed a reign of terror
Pillaging villages, robbing and killing passers-by.
Brave Theseus knowingly took that perilous way,
Encountered these bandits and killed all of them.
So, people hailed him as their savior, and his fame
As a worthy prince had already spread far and near
By the time he presented himself before his father.
King Aegeus could recognize his illustrious son
When he saw his own sword and what he put on.
It must have been a touching scene; for the father
And the son, for the first time, gazed at each other.

Theseus basked in his glory; his luck was on a rise;
But he noticed certain things, which made him sad.
He saw some citizens moving with downcast eyes;
They blinked back tears, drifting around like mad.
When he asked those people: "What is the matter?"
They averted their eyes, with: "Do ask your father."

"Why not you?" he urged them; but no reply came.
He reflected: "Only when a country's secret shame
Is interlinked with that country's woe and calamity,
People suffer a lot, but do not feel like discussing it."

Finally, his father briefed him about the sad incident,
Adding: 'Now we have to send the fresh contingent
Of fourteen youngsters whom a monster will devour.
I know it's a bribe to prevent another Cretan invasion.
It's demoralizing, true, but it is less harmful than war.
We all know what a war does to the defeated nation."

The harrowing account touched Theseus to the quick.
It humbled his pride; it made him trenchant and sick.
Then and there, he announced his firm determination
To be another victim with the young women and men
Who, very unwillingly, but under patriotic compulsion,
Were prepared to meet their end in the Minotaur's den
In order to save their beloved Athens from destruction.

The old king Aegeus tried to dissuade Theseus.
His unhappy countrymen collectively opposed,
But the prince insisted that he'd no other options.
He argued: "The king and his heir are supposed
To safeguard their state's well-being and honour,
And to do their best to protect people from danger.
That apart, my only purpose is to kill the Minotaur
Not to die. This practice shouldn't continue forever."
Though Theseus's brave words pleased his people,
They knew the Minotaur was not just another bull.
They ardently requested him to change his decision.
But then again, he was not just another young man.

Theseus reached the Cretan island with all his crew.
When they were paraded in front of Minos's throne,
Ariadne, the princess saw them, and her heart grew
Very soft. When she zeroed in on the young scion
Theseus, her sad, compassionate heart missed a beat,
And so she was resolute to do something to avert it.
It was, indeed, too painful for that princess to bear
That fourteen Athenians in the first flush of youth,
Brought up with so much affection, hope and care
By their parents, should enter a monster's mouth.
Determined to avert the disaster, she quickly met
With Daedalus, and gained upon the ace architect

Who confided to the kind princess the simple ways
One can make good his escape from that mizmaze.
Then she arranged a secret meeting with Theseus
And gave him a bundle of thread and useful tip-offs
About how to come out of that dark and dangerous
Labyrinth if he succeeded in slaying the Minotaur.
"Tie one end of the thread," she said, "to the pillar
At the gate, and carry the ball of thread unwinding
It as you move deeper and deeper into that building.

The Minotaur is strong, but if you luckily survive it,
Cautiously follow the thread to the Labyrinth's exit."

Prince Theseus thanked the noble-hearted princess
For her concern for them and her timely assistance.
Next day they were pushed into the maw of horrors.
Its inner layout was actually an architectural wonder,
With a mind-blowing network of identical corridors
That intermingled with, and intersected one another;
Steep, tall walls hedged the corridors and ran parallel.
And the ubiquitous presence of the predatory monster
Made that murky and confined place more diabolical.

The corridors of the Labyrinth were zigzag and dim,
And the stalking beast could take any period of time
To discover, frolic with and devour the human victim.
The beast could spring into action and pounce on him
From behind, in front, from above, from left and right,
And the victim's waiting was tortuous, full of anxiety.
The prowling and shadowy presence of that monster
Was a relentless foreboding: anytime and anywhere.
Inside the Labyrinth there was no light, no victuals,
That made the plight of the victims truly horrendous.

Ere the ball of yarn unwound itself, Theseus located
The Minotaur. He told his mates to stand at a remove.
He pounced on the beast suddenly. It never suspected
That any one would dare to attack it. It bristled, strove
To stand up, but Theseus pinned it down to the ground.
The monster wriggled and produced a bellowing sound.

Theseus took it by the horns, and sitting astride its back,
Applying his full strength, he twisted and broke its neck.

Mother Nature smiled through radiant flowers
And darkness of the night unburdened its fears
When the monster yielded to the power of man,
Sending out his dying and spine-chilling groan.
Ariadne was waiting for them at the gate anxiously.
They, following the thread, emerged triumphantly.
They longed for new adventures; they were game.
But she advised them to quickly repair to the port.
She told them that her royal father would do them
What that Labyrinth and the Minotaur could not.
She warned them that they'd good reasons to fear
The king's retributive anger, because that Minotaur
Was his stepson after all, though from his wife's side.
"You mainland Greeks my father heartily despised,"
She said, "Because your king first violated the rule
By sending my brother Androgeos to harness a bull.
You must admit, he lost his only son because of you.
Now you dispatched his queen's son Minotaur, too.
You have to make off with your life ere it is too late.
 If you delay your escape, you will tempt your Fate."

Prince Theseus was charmed by her noble nature,
And expressed his earnest intention to marry her.
But Ariadne politely and firmly declined his offer
With: "Though I know you'd be a brave husband,
Nevertheless, Theseus, I know one thing for sure
That your grateful heart makes you seek my hand.
I helped you out of kindness not of a selfish desire.
I know a bond born of gratitude won't long endure.
Medea, helped Jason to achieve the Golden Fleece;
But he ditched her ungratefully, you know all this."

Some writers bruited an untrue and most malicious
Rumour that Ariadne eloped with her lover Theseus
Who, though grateful, was not genuinely fond of her,
And so he soon marooned her on a deserted shore.
They are baseless canards! And it stands to reason

That a blue-blooded hero could never be so mean.
It's also most unlikely and incredible that Theseus
Who always fought and risked his life for strangers,
Who was magnanimous, noble-natured and so kind
Could be so bad as to leave his benefactress behind.

****

The Chimaera and Bellerophon

The Echidna was the child of Gaeae and Tartarus;
She was a female monster, half snake, half woman.
She had produced two quite well known monsters,
The Hydra and the Chimaera, by lying with Typhon.

The Chimaera was a scary and patchwork creature.
 Many animals were brazed together to fashion her.
She possessed the fuzzy head of a full-grown lion.
Her prehensile tail was a cobra or a boa constrictor.
A goat's head on her back looked like a decoration.
She had the fanciful make of a patchwork monster.
She lived on the peak of a cloud-kissing mountain
On the outskirts of Corinth, also known as Ephyra.
The Chimaera carried on her predation in the plain.
Like her ravenous sibling sister the Hydra of Lerna,
She ravaged the countryside to satisfy her hunger.
And people of Corinth were mortally afraid of her.

Now, a boy was growing like an obsession
In a not-so-distinguished family in Corinth,
Like a pine rearing itself quietly in seclusion
From the tough interior of the mother earth.
This child grew up and became Bellerophon
Who was famous for his fierce determination.

It was the time when Corinth was ruled by Glaucus.
He was the son of a hero manqué named Sisyphus
Whose name is latterly linked up with Albert Camus.
This author redeemed Sisyphus's dubious reputation
By likening his ordeals to man's existential condition.

This fabled king was passionately infatuated with life;
He was in love with power, was in love with his wife.
Being a mortal, he died one day; and then as a spirit
He entered the Hades, a place he never liked to visit.

To the god of the Underworld he made a supplication
That he'd died suddenly leaving some jobs half done
And that if he is given an opportunity to return again
To the Earth, he'd finish his jobs and come back fain.
Pluto, who had full control over the spirits of the dead,
Believed him, and, going out of his way, he accorded
Him his wish. He finished his jobs but went on living;
Pluto sent reminders, but the king was past all caring.
He tried to circumvent his death by hook or by crook,
So, he infuriated the gods by such an obsessive outlook.
When all attempts failed, Hermes took him by force
To Hades, or he was brained by the thunder of Zeus

The Chimaera

Gods had to inflict on him an exemplary punishment
So that he'd learn a lesson while enduring his torment.
To wise him up to the meaning of human existence,

Pluto carried him to the hilly outskirts of the Hades.
"It's my order", Zeus decreed, "You push this rock
Up to the summit of that yonder precipitous hillock.
Mind you, Sisyphus, until and unless you fix it there
You won't hope of having a break from your labour.
The type of life you crazy mortals lead in the world
Always chasing mirages of power, lusting for gold,
Getting tanked up on pleasures, fighting over trifles,
Robbing the weak, cheating others without scruples,
Compromising on everything to gratify your desire,
All the time sniffing around for the grubs of pleasure,
Proves one thing: that you're a mob of stupid blokes,
Not knowing you are the butt of our practical jokes.
So this rock will be your torment and your scripture
To teach you the ultimate end of human endeavour."

The programmed rock won't stay put on one place;
When it touches the top, it'd start its downhill race.
That push-and-roll-game, perhaps, is still going on
Though Sisyphus had long since learnt that lesson
And transmitted that to us, in an attractive package,
Through Albert Camus, a maverick sage of our age.
The hero manqué loves not his job, nor does he hate,
Nor has he completely reconciled himself to his fate.
Still he slogs it out pushing the rock up and again up.
He is not driven to despair, because he does not hope.
He passes on a message through his stoical suffering
That even if life is absurd, man has to keep on living;
That man is a condemned creature in God's vast zoo,
For him there is no way out, nor round, nor through;
That a thinking mortal can steal a march on his Boss
By eschewing the fruit of actions, by being conscious.

That message of Sisyphus' was a sobering one,
But it was taken curiously by Glaucus, his son.
If man's life on earth, he reasoned, is so absurd,
There is nothing wrong if men want to play God.
He deviously tampered with the natural process
By offering human beings as fodder to his horses.

Gods frowned on Glaucus for his inhuman deeds.
One day he was devoured alive by his own steeds.

Now it's time we reverted to our prime narration
Concerning that illustrious youth, Bellerophon
Who was believed to be Glaucus's secret son,
Because he was so prince-like and handsome.
His only companion was his mother Eurynome,
Who was, unfortunately, an unmarried woman.
That was why, there was a general speculation
About her mysterious paramour and the father
Of such an extraordinarily ambitious youngster:
Whether king Glaucus, or the sea-god Poseidon.
But Athena's conscientious and caring attention
To Eurynome attested to the hearsay that her son
Was consanguine to the ancient god of the ocean.

Bellerohon had an ambition of a very special kind.
And so people thought he had gone out of his mind.
The young dude aspired to make Pegasus his mount.
That white horse rose from the blood of the Gorgon
And from his hoof-puddle flowed the famous fount
Hippocrene sacred to the Muses on the Mt. Helicon.
The water of that spring could bestow poetic vision.
Pegasus was heavenly, a proud possession of Zeus;
So it was as much a sacrilege to hope for that horse
As a human conqueror trying to colonize Parnassus.
Besides, that flying horse had not yet been broken
Or harnessed, or mounted by any other god or man.

Man has a divine soul, that everybody says;
And he hurtles in space like a load of matter,
Dark, inchoate, shapeless; only when the rays
Of the sun of aspiration, either remote or near,
Illumes it, it looks bright as a moon or a comet.
Man is as big as his dream, as it sculpts his fate.
It has also been conclusively proved quite often
That if the aspirant is a noble and earnest man,
And his aspirations are life-friendly and grand,
If they are backed up by the appropriate action,

The gods regard him with grudging admiration
And extend, to that aspirant, their helping hand.
Bellerophon, well advised by prophet Polydus,
Sought Athena's blessings through meditation.
And the goddess helped him out of his impasse
By visiting him in his dream. She told him thus:
"Are you asleep? Now you wake up, young man.
Cheer up! Your father is no other than Poseidon.
You are very ambitious, your aim is determinate.
So I give you a gift. It may get you what you covet."

Bellerophon woke up to reality. It was the middle
Of the night. He looked around and found a bridle
Lying close to his bed. It was made of purest gold
The like of which he hadn't seen, so nice to behold.
He lifted the bridle, thrilled to the nocturnal silence;
Walking to the meadows, he peered into the glades.
At a little distance he discovered a strange presence.
A big horse with an eagle's wings and golden mane
Was drinking water from a fountain known as Pirene.
He approached him cautiously with great excitement.
When Pegasus found him with Athena's instrument,
He was surprised, and quietly suffered to be bridled
By a human. Bellerophon got him carefully saddled.

The flying horse was actually a dream come true.
Bellerophon mounted him and experienced a new
Feeling, zipping through broad regions of the sky,
Now moving in a canter, suddenly shooting up high.
Old men blessed him; people viewed him with awe.
He wanted to perform miracles; he was raring to go.

Man on this shifting earth stands all the time under
A cosmic wind-mill set up by goddess Moira, where
One phase of well-being is broken and torn asunder
By the bludgeoning of the eternally rotating structure.

Things for Bellerophon took an unpleasant turn,
And he became the saddest man under the sun.

In the circumstances not very elaborately stated,
He inadvertently did something he never wanted
To do: he caused the death of one of his brothers.
So, for purification, he went to the ruler of Argos.
The ritual of purification was time-taking process.
And he had to spend a month in Proetus's palace.
King Proetus had a pretty wife called Stheneboea.
Homer and Hesiod gave her another name: Anteia.
Our hero was dashingly handsome, but a bit prim.
It so happened that the queen had a crush on him,
When she supped and chatted up with the stranger.
Her passionate desire overpowered her discretion;
One night, that queen dressed in her birthday attire,
Summoned him to her bedroom. Finding the man
Too naive, she revealed to him her heart's desire

When a married woman with youth and beauty
Becomes voracious, and is given to promiscuity,
A desire for the forbidden joy gets into her head,
And she scorns to waste her loveliness, possibility
And sweet charms on the desert of a marriage-bed.

But noble Bellerophon politely declined her offer;
Her declared availability had no effect on the hero.
So naturally, she became revengeful in her shame,
Went to her husband Proetus, and threw the blame:
"That horny youth from Corinth", she tearfully lied,
"Has tried to usurp your right on our marriage bed."

The angry king wanted to do away with the sinner,
But he realized it would be improper to kill a guest
Who had already shared with him many a dinner.
"If you're so punctilious", she pressed her request,
"Why don't you dispatch that sinner to my father
With a sealed letter containing your instruction?
My father will kill him for outraging his daughter."
Proetus was relieved and made a wry observation:
"You women are certainly God's zaniest creation;
You cause problems, but you know the solution."

Bellerophon and Pegasus

Of all the monsters Nature has set on humanity,
None can surpass a spurned woman in brutality.
That was what Astydamia, the sly wife of Acastus
Had done to Peleus, the father of the hero Achilles.
Phaedra, the adulterous spouse of noble Theseus,
Committed suicide to ruin her stepson Hippolytus,
Who was steadfast in virtue and a man of honour,
So, chose filial duty to love and spurned her offer.
The virtuous have ever had a tough time to reply
To the fusillades of false charges, to such mishaps;
History's marketplace always had a steady supply
Of Pontiphar's wives and such victimized Josephs.

Thus instigated by his "outraged" wife Stheneboea,
The king sent our hero to Iobates, the king of Lysia.
With the swift-flying Pegasus at his beck and call,
Covering long distance posed him no problem at all.
He took the missive, mounted his horse with delight,
And reached the king's palace in less than an hour.
King Iobates treated him with friendly hospitality.
Nine full days he shared with his guest his dinner.
On the tenth day, the king cared to read the letter
That his son-in-law Proetus sent him. As he read it,
He was aghast at the sheer magnitude of the guilt

His guest had committed; so he thought it proper
To send Bellerophon, without delay, to his Maker.

But, once again, that sacrosanct host-guest bond
Prevented him from straightaway killing the man.
Besides, that king had already grown quite fond
Of his well-mannered guest. So, he devised a plan
To kill Bellerophon without violating the tradition.

"Well, young chap." he said: "you might have heard
Of a monster called the Chimaera. I'd be very glad
If you slew it, but it may not be within your power."
"O, Chimaera!" said the hero: "She is my neighbour.
I hail from Corinth, you know. I haven't yet seen her,
But I've heard that she dwells somewhere near there.
They say she is an invincible beast, very dangerous.
Let me see if I can kill her with my ordinary arrows.
While fighting with the Chimaera, if I meet my end,
O king, pray for me and remember me as a friend."

Then, he rode off sitting astraddle on his Pegasus
With his bow and quiver of bronze-tipped arrows.
Bellerophon had no trouble locating the monster,
As the horse knew everything; he took him there.

The Chimaera, a huge predator, stood like a cliff
On the wooded slope of a hill, holding in her grip
A full-grown mountain caribou she had picked up
From the jungle, and was climbing up to the top
Of the hill, when an arrow struck her on the back.
Surprised and vexed, the beast dropped her prey,
Looked up, saw the flying horse and tried to attack
The horse and his rider, sending out a loud war cry,
Lifting her hissing tail, but she came badly unstuck
Because, the horse Pegasus was flying safely high.
She was visible, because she was taller than a tree.

Bellerophon, sitting pretty, was on a shooting spree.
Pointed arrows pierced through her flanks and neck.
She searched in vain for a cover. "For Hera's sake,"

Cried she, "Stop shooting these arrows from the air.
Come to the earth, man. Let's have a fair encounter.
You reach me, I cannot reach you; it's not so fair."
"It seems," Bellerophon joked, "You are not yet aware
That everything is alright in matters of love and war."
And she: "Then, if some timid crows will kill a viper
By pecking, does it prove that the crows are stronger?"
"You talk of fairness?" He retorted: "That's a shame!
Are you fair to your victims when you devour them?"

A couple of well-aimed arrows cut off the Python.
The Chimaera bled profusely, looked chap-fallen.
Sitting astride Pegasus, Bellerophon bravely fought.
Finally, he killed the Chimaera, the fierce offspring
Of Echidna. His conquest over what people thought
Invincible pleased and disappointed the Lysian king.
Though the king appreciated the courage of the hero,
He could not forgive him for outraging his daughter.
Once again, Iobates ordered his guest to wage a war
Against the Amazons, a tribe of belligerent women.
After conquering the amazons, he came back again
To the king; he wanted to be put to some new labour,
Desiring to give expression to his spirit of adventure.
After knowing Bellerophon well, the king was certain
That such a noble youth couldn't have raped a woman.
Maybe, the laudable actions of that former-day Houdini
Had convinced the Lysian king of latter's divine origin.

The king changed his mind; to make up for his error,
He gave him a half of his kingdom, and his daughter.

When a laudable aspiration takes wrong roads
And degenerates into an unholy lust for power,
The aspirant loses his self-control, and the gods
Wax indignant and review him with displeasure.
It's reported that Bellerophon became a bit sassy,
After living peaceably for a good number of years.
One day, he was possessed with a fantastic fancy
And bade his divine and fast-flying horse Pegasus
To transport him to the top of the mount Olympus

Where he'd have the pleasure of dining with Zeus.
Pegasus realized that Bellerophon had gone insane,
Because, such hospitality was not extended to men.
So instead of obeying his command, he dropped
Bellerophon from the saddle and quickly hopped
It out of the earth and entered the stables of Zeus.
The last few years of this dashing and glamorous
Hero were spent in repentance and utter despair
As a result of that one instance of misdemeanor.

****

The Sphinx and Oedipus

The Sphinx, it seems, was a reasonable monster,
Because she used to allow her victims an option:
If one can give her a correct answer, he kills her;
If his reply is incorrect, he will meet destruction.
.

The Sphinx's award of punishment was too cruel:
She will die if you pass and you will die if you fail.
As she posed her question as a pretext for murder,
All her victims were undone by their fear of failure.
Her question was not so profound, only a bit clever:
He, who'd solve her puzzle, was a 'double' gainer:
Because, he would not only make his own escape,
But kill her as well and become the ruler of Thebes.

Some monsters killed people by sheer brute force.
Some others, sensibly, gave their victims a chance.
The Sirens say: "If you don't love our song, get lost.
But if you happen to love our songs, come you must."
The Sphinx says: "If you perchance prove cleverer,
You will survive and I shall dash against this pillar."
We may not find fault with the conditions of her bet;
Her fault was: she compelled people to take the test.

The family story of the Sphinx is very nebulous;
And at certain stages, it may appear incestuous.
It all started with the Echidna, a female dragon.
Upper half of her body was like that of a woman,
In the lower half of her body, she was a python,
Thrashing about in the holes of the marshy earth,
Devouring her victims raw, spreading desolation,
Killing creatures that ventured to cross her path.
The Echidna bore to Typhoeus two other monsters.
One of them was the hound of the Hades, Cerberus;
The other, a two-headed spaniel known as Orthros.
Then Echidna mated with Orthros, canine fashion,
And gave birth to the Sphinx and the Nemean Lion.

Sphinx

The family story of the Sphinx is very nebulous;
And at certain stages, it may appear incestuous.
It all started with the Echidna, a female dragon.
Upper half of her body was like that of a woman,
In the lower half of her body, she was a python,
Thrashing about in the holes of the marshy earth,
Devouring her victims raw, spreading desolation,
Killing creatures that ventured to cross her path.

The Echidna bore to Typhoeus two other monsters.
One of them was the hound of the Hades, Cerberus;
The other, a two-headed spaniel known as Orthros.
Then Echidna mated with Orthros, canine fashion,
And gave birth to the Sphinx and the Nemean Lion.

The Sphinx had wings, but the torso of a lioness;
Like a woman, she had long hair and a pretty face.
Such a blend of features was capable of arousing
Amorphous feelings of attraction, and of loathing.

To meet her, a youth wended his way homewards
Led by an inscrutable fate: His name was Oedipus.

No one tried more than him to be sinless and noble,
But none was made to commit actions more sinful.

For our readers' information, we will a little digress
To tell the tragic tale of a man who fell from grace.
Laius, then, was the king of the city-state of Thebes.
Being sexually deviant, he'd incurred a family curse.
Years ago, he'd betrayed the trust of his host Pelops
By seducing and abducting latter's son Chrysippus.
Laius emulated such examples as were set by the gods:
Zeus's crush for Ganymede, Apollo's for Hyacinthus.
But the gods didn't take kindly to Laius for that action.
Seducing pretty boys, for them, was just a diversion,
But for Laius, an earthling, it was sexual perversion.

For many years, Laius and Jocasta didn't have a heir.
So they went to Apollo's shrine to know their future.
The Oracle of Apollo warned the curious king, Laius
That Jocasta'd bear a son, not as a boon but as a curse.
For their son would kill his father and wed his mother.
The horrified king planned to scotch those predictions
By killing the child while young to stave off a disaster.
The son was born, and when he was a little child,
The king spiked his foot and threw him in the wild

To be devoured by animals. In vain the king tried
To alter his fate, for the Oracle of Apollo never lied.

A Corinthian shepherd, while tending king's flock,
Saw the child and took it to his own king, Polybus.
The king was childless; so he thought it good luck.
He nurtured him as his son; he called him Oedipus,
Meaning "a swollen foot," as his foot was swollen.
Months passed, then years; time was marching on;
The child Oedipus grew and became a young man
Always believing that he was the child of Polybus.

Once, as the luck would have it, he grew curious
To know his future, and consulted Apollo's Sybil.
She told him that he was the man who would kill

His father and commit another preposterous crime
By marrying his own mother in due course of time.

He mused: "Why on earth must I commit such sins?
Killing father to become king is a barbarous means.
Marrying my mother? It stings like a scorpion's tail.
Have all our unmarried pretty damsels gone to hell?
I have no such pathological craze for sex and power.
Such sins can frighten even the world's worst sinner.
I have a will of my own. I'll do only what I deem fit.
Who on Earth or in heaven would compel me into it?"

But when he gave the prophesy a careful thought
His confidence sagged and he suffered a bad jolt.
The Oracles of Apollo, he reasoned, are infallible.
That realization made him tense and lose his cool.
"Gods," he mused, "are shrewd, scheming writers
Of the book of life and we men are just characters.
Can a character rise above the author's intention?
By Zeus, it is an unlikely and impossible situation.
Can't I succeed, then, in doing what I decide to do?
Of man's Freewill and the requirements of his Fate,
Which one of them is an illusion, which one is true?"
As he deliberated, he broke out into a cold sweat.
His heart palpitated, he saw stars, his head swam,
And the blood in his veins started flowing faster.
Fear hit the citadel of his will like a battering ram.
And he decided to flee from his father and mother.

Oedipus fled from Corinth, determined not to return
So long as his own parents lived. He was on the run.
He tried to dodge Fate, but it chased him as a hunter.
On his way, he had an encounter with an old stranger
Who was riding in a royal chariot; his hair was hoary.
He was attended to by a retinue of guards with livery.
A hot exchange of words soon turned to a bloody one,
 And Oedipus killed all of them save a single minion.
That survivor who witnessed the murder of the king
Would play later on a crucial role in the unraveling.
He was forced to kill the old man to save his honour.

Later on, he came to know that he was his real father.
For several years, he wandered listless like a fugitive,
Debating with himself whether to live, or not to live
In a place where Fate undermines man's intention.
In fine, he was a victim of an existential depression.
While crossing the outskirts of the Theban kingdom,
He talked with some locals and got the information
About a certain monster that held the city to ransom.
He heard that the protector of Thebes named Creon
Had declared that the man who could kill the monster
Would become the king and marry Jocasta, his sister.
The Sphinx, he gathered, was an oddity, a flying lion,
With animal ferocity and bodily features of a woman.
The people of Thebes also informed young Oedipus
That none could kill the Sphinx with a sword or spear,
Because, like all monsters, she'd supernatural powers,
But by challenging and proving intellectually superior;
That the only way to do away with that pedantic bully
Was to answer the question she would pose correctly.
Oedipus, moronic as he was, wanted to take a chance.
"If I die", thought he, "that would be a good riddance.
And if I succeed in killing the Sphinx, well and good;
I shall be of some use, and that will restore my mood."

He approached the Sphinx, primed for interrogation.
Sitting on a tower, she watched him with compassion,
And said thus: "I guess, you are a moronic young man,
Disenchanted, a bum suffering from acute malnutrition,
Who would be glad to die. Though I am quite capable
Of killing any one I want to, I don't do so on principle.
I do not kill a worthy person, but I cannot suffer a fool.
Now answer me, who is that creature that has four feet
In the morning; in high noon, it walks about on just two
And becomes a three-legged scarecrow in the twilight?
Come out with a correct answer, or I shall devour you."
"It is rather simple", answered resourceful Oedipus;
"The creature you mean is man, he moves on all fours
In his infancy; most of his life he walks on his two feet,
And when he gets old, he uses a stick as a walking-kit;
Then his leg joints get weak, and he becomes decrepit.

Your riddle is witty, but in certain cases that is wrong:
We see men die in their infacy and even when young.
A young man if he is lame or rickety may use a crutch
And children hop on one leg when they play hopscotch.
We see old men stride to their graves, full of high-jinx.
They will clobber you, if you offer them walking sticks."

On hearing that answer, the Sphinx turned pale.
She fluttered her wings and rose slap like a gale
High up into the air, and descended very rapidly
With a menacing death-wish and dashed violently
Her pretty woman's head against that same tower
On which she perched. It was the end of a monster
Who proved by dying that she was a fair gambler.
The people of Thebes hailed Oedipus as their king,
Because he, by destroying the Sphinx, could bring
Peace to the kingdom. He wedded the widow-queen,
As that bond was needed to establish his royal line.
Oedipus proved his worth both as a man and a ruler,
His foes feared him; to his citizens he was a father.

He solved the Sphinx's riddle, but the riddle of Fate
Turned out to be more pernicious and more intricate.
Ignorantly he went on enjoying the life of such incest
As ordinary mortals run away from, and the gods hate.
He innocently believed all the time that he had foiled
The designs of Fate, but the inexorable Fate coiled
On him like a large boa constrictor, and crushed him.

Oedipus's desire to know his future, and his decision
To influence events was a part of the greater scheme,
And his foreknowledge only sped up his destruction.
Finally, his life's inscrutable bobbin unwound itself
And soon the dark and macabre secrets were known:
Jocasta, both his mother and his wife, hanged herself
When she realized her husband was her begotten son.
And Oedipus was ashamed of wearing his own eyes
Which did not enable him to recognize such disgrace.
Therefore, he scooped out his eyes with his own nails
And, led by Antigone, went to a sanctuary in Athens.

The Story of the Centaurs

War god Mars (Greeks called him Ares) had a son
Who was a bit of a reprobate; his name was Ixion.
While Ixion lived as a guest in the house of Jupiter,
He went utterly crazy and nursed on unholy desire
For no less a person than Juno, the Queen Consort.
And Jupiter, alas, finally came to know about that.
But, instead of getting angry, he was vastly amused
To find in his upstart guest such a libidinal fortitude.
He possibly did not like to condemn such lewdness
In Ixion, and to sermonize on virtues and continence,
Because he himself was not free from such frivolity
And had never attached importance to marital fidelity.
He wondered how one could be so saucy and so bold
As to try to make him, the ace philanderer, a cuckold.

A Fighting Centaur

In order to play upon Ixion's misplaced passion,
He formed a white cloud in the likeness of Juno
And, with a generous smile, proffered it to Ixion.
They mated. Out of that fantastical consummation
Was born a full-grown monster called Centaurus.
No sooner was he born than he made a lot of fuss,
Romped around fired with uncontrollable desires,
And found in the mares of Pelion his sex partners.

Centaurus, by these mares, sired a herd of centaurs
Who possessed great strength and unusual features.
Each had a horse's body topped with a human head.
As equine and human creatures, a dual life they led,
Having man's mind and horse's power and passion.

A diabolical lot, they were cunning, virile and strong.
Rarely they did anything right, but always did wrong.
They formed the cortege of the orgiastic god Bacchus
And reveled with the nymphs, priapi, sileni and satyrs.

Once upon a time, a famous Centaur called Eurytion
Was invited, by the Lepiths, to a marriage reception.
He drank a lot of hard drinks and became very wild,
Bullied hosts, blustered and tried to abduct the bride.
When resisted, the Centaur began to neigh and yelp;
In no time, hundreds of Centaurs rushed to his help,
Brandishing swords, bronze clubs and uprooted oaks.
They spoilt the nuptial feast and terrorized the folks.
That skirmish between the Lepiths and the Centaurs
Was a fierce one and it continued for several hours.
Thanks to Theseus (who luckily was present there,)
And many invited dignitaries and legendary heroes,
The barbarous hoard of the Centaurs came a cropper
And they were sent packing to the frontiers of Epirus.

There was one centaur whose name was Nessus.
He was a raunchy creature; he became notorious
For having accelerated the apotheosis of Hercules.
Hercules met him on the bank of the river Evanus.

He greeted him and said: "Nessus, how do you do?
If you are in no hurry, please do me a favor or two.
Meet Deineira my wife; she is not a good swimmer.
I would you carried her across this brimming river."
Nessus obliged him, but when they were halfway
Across the river, the Centaur molested his charge.
Standing on the bank, Hercules heard his wife cry.
Such misconduct irked him and aroused his gorge.
Shooting a poisoned arrow he injured the offender.
Though fatally hurt, he carried her across the river,
Before dying, he gave her a tunic wet with his blood,
Saying: "This magic cloth is for Hercules, your lord.

Preserve it. Whenever you feel his love for you wilt,
Gift him this charmed tunic, and ask him to wear it."

Several years after, Hercules put on that fatal tunic
Sent by Deineira. She unwittingly used it as a tonic
To regain her husband's love and affection for her.
She was justly jealous. Besides what's a charm for,
If it is not used at the moment of a conjugal crisis?
The poisoned tunic burnt into the body of Hercules,
Speeding up his desired, but excruciating apotheosis.
That unhappy incident may serve as an eye-opener
To all good wives, husbands and lovers world over
Who are prone to, or suffer from, mutual suspicion
That can be as potent a killer as the Hydra's poison.

One fine day Atalanta, the warlike daughter of Iasus,
Was taking a walk in the forest with bow and arrows.
Her rugged beauty maddened two lustful Centaurs.
They stalked her. She could sense their intentions.
When they tried to assault her, she shot them down
Without much ado and wended her way to the town.

Chiron, the Centaur

There was another centaur: he was good and great.
His name was Chiron, a great savant of many parts,
Who, by many noble deeds, was able to recuperate
The loss of reputation of his tribe, to erase the blots
Of shame caused by the misdeeds of some upstarts.
He lived in his woodland academy on a sloping hill.
He had the beautiful body of a snow-white stallion,
Gifted with a sage's mind and a heart that could feel.
His bearded face shone with wisdom and compassion.
He was far above the amatory and ordinary passions
Which bedevilled other Centaurs and many humans.
He taught his pupils civic manners, the art of warfare,
The arts of healing the sick, of playing up on the lyre.
He trained them in gymnastics, in many other sports,
In trekking rough terrains, in rowing ships and boats,
In wrestling and boxing, in harnessing unruly mares,
And in using weapons, such as, swords and spears.
Like the versatile gurus of India in the ancient age,
He trained them how to rule kingdoms and to graze
Kine and sheep. Chiron might have excelled in the art
Of tending cows and sheep and imparting that lesson,
Because a Centaur etymologically refers to an expert
In rounding up livestock, particularly sheep and oxen.
A Centaur, in fact, is horse and rider welded into one.

Chiron the Centaur, it is said, had learnt his many arts
From Athena, Apollo, Hermes and the war-god Mars.
Some of the heroes who'd graduated from his academe
Were legends in their lifetime and rose to great fame.

Achilles was his student. That unconquerable Achilles!
A darling of the Olympians, born of Peleus and Thetis!
Of all the big heroes who joined the Trojan expedition,
Achilles was rated the greatest by far. He struck terror
In the enemy ranks and killed the Trojan hero Hector.
In Homeric saga, Achilles occupies a distinct position
Comparable to that of the Mahabharata prince Arjuna.

Chiron taught Aesculapius the skill of curing the sick,
Of healing the wounded. His recipes acted like magic
On the dying patients, and could strengthen the weak.
Theseus was his disciple, who began his heroic feats
By completely exterminating several gangs of bandits.
The greatest landmark of Theseus's illustrious career:
He entered the Cretan labyrinth and killed the Minotaur.

Jason graduated from Chiron's woodland institution.
He was a celebrated hero with an iron determination.
He voyaged with his forty-nine comrades to Colchis,
Yoked the brazen bulls of Vulcan, eluded the dragon
And was able to bring the Golden Fleece to Greece.

That polymath Chiron was also a virtuoso musician
Who taught Orpheus how to play on the harp Aeolian.
It is reported that Orpheus, by his music, could enthrall
Pluto, the king of the under world. He notched up a win
Against the Sirens, rendering them defunct once for all.
He was a great charmer like the Pied Piper of Hamelyn.

According to some classical sources of information,
Hercules learnt wrestling and archery from Chiron.
Once the teacher and the disciple fell out of favour,
And Hercules, with a toxic arrow, injured his teacher.
The wound did not heal, and it gave him a lot of pain.
As he was immortal, he couldn't die like normal men.

So, he gifted his immortality, with the consent of Zeus,
To the noble benefactor of mankind, Titan Prometheus.

Chiron, that noble and accomplished horse-cum-man,
By his exemplary achievements taught us all a lesson
That it is wrong to judge a human being or a Centaur,
In terms of their species, or creed, or clan, or gender.

****

Children of Zeus through different goddesses and women:

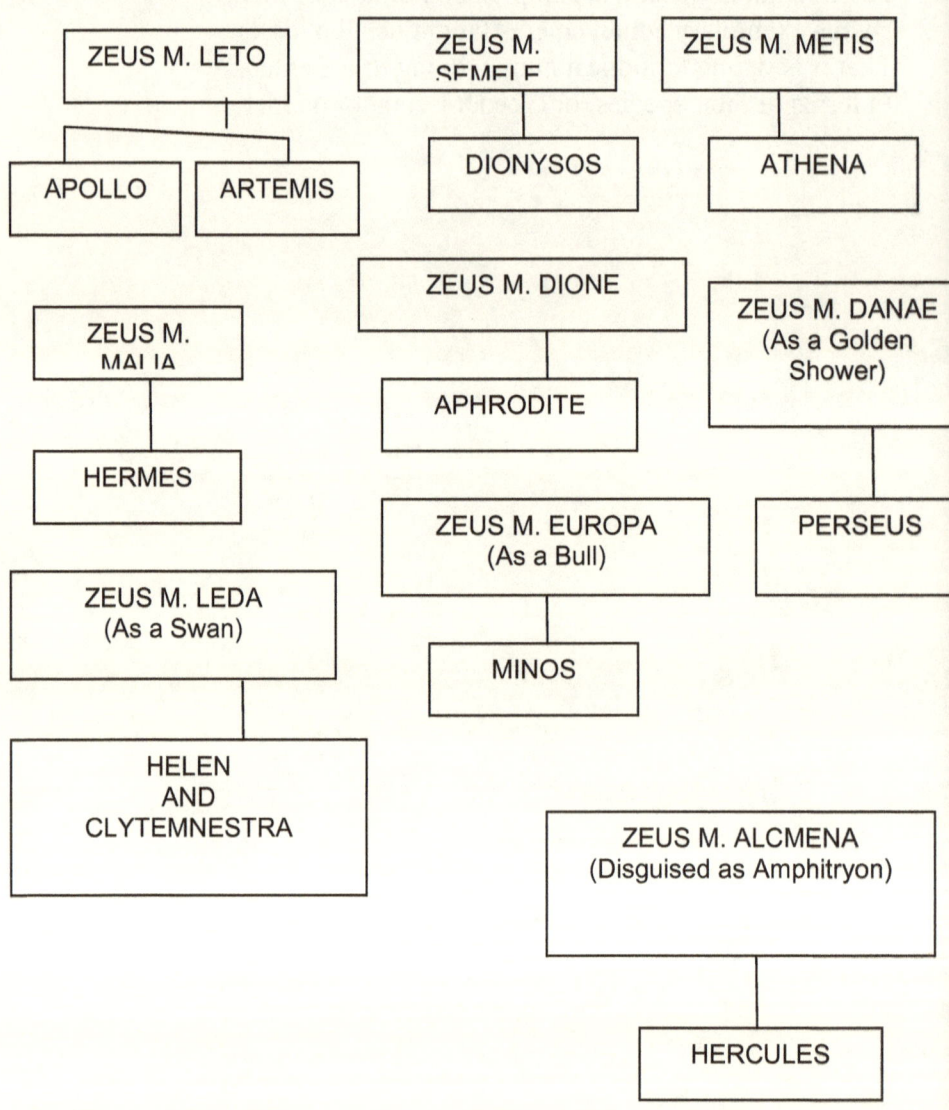

www.ingramcontent.com/pod-product-compliance
Lightning Source LLC
Chambersburg PA
CBHW050830180626
46814CB00004B/1545